BENEATH THE BARS OF JUSTICE

A Historical Work of Fiction

By
Bailey-Bankston

DEDICATION

To my family, especially my mother, Louise Bailey Webb,
for supporting me in all my endeavors throughout the
years, and to my 66 cell mates in the Camilla, Georgia, city
jail who were courageous and determined in their fight
for freedom and who gave me the strength to cross the
finish line.

Special thanks and a debt of gratitude to Marilyn Ellison-Pounsel, my lifetime confidante, for reviewing and editing not just this novel but its earlier version almost 25 years ago.

In memory of Dad, my four grandparents,
and brother, Charles

CHAPTER ONE

My name is Savannah-Belle. There is no hyphen or space separating my name on my birth certificate. It was not until I was well into adulthood that I began hyphenating my name, around the time women began hyphenating their married and surnames. It was trendy and, in my mind, taking this liberty with my given name took the sting out of having such an old-fashioned name. You see, I carry the names of both my grandmothers, Savannah and Belle. I always thought it was too much of a burden for a child to bear. Both were very religious and righteous women, and I knew that I would bring shame to their names if I ever did anything disrespectful or immoral, and heaven forbid, anything unlawful. So, it seemed to me that I tip-toed through a lot of my childhood because of the "honor" that had been bestowed upon my life by carrying those two names.

I reasoned that my mother called me by both names because she didn't want it to appear that she favored her mother's name, Savannah, over my dad's mother's name, Belle. My dad, on the other hand, called me Noodle. He said he coined this nickname for me because I looked like a long, wet spaghetti noodle when I was born. That name stayed with me throughout my childhood, although it was shortened to just Noo after a few years. Only my dad and siblings called me Noo, and although I grew to tolerate it, they knew not to call me Noo outside the walls of our family home. Not even my closest friends knew about this name.

I was very curious as a child and wanted to be involved in everything happening in the world around me. I was even called a busybody at times, and I think that was pretty descriptive of my personality, my demeanor, and who I was.

During the summer of 1962, when I was 13 years old and preparing to enter the 9th grade, my last year of junior high school, I began attending some of the Civil Rights Movement's Monday night mass meetings at Shiloh Baptist Church in my hometown of Albany, Georgia. Everybody was going to those meetings. The movement had been organized several months earlier because of the need to address issues and civil unrest in the Negro community. The mass meetings consisted of a lot of singing and talking about freedom and injustice. Some people already had been arrested for marching into downtown Albany to demonstrate against the way Negroes were being treated.

In fact, about 6 months earlier, before school recessed for the Christmas holidays, several students from Albany State College had been expelled from school for marching for their rights. It was all everybody talked about. And all the teenagers were now getting involved because we were out of school for summer vacation and could fully participate. So, naturally, I wanted to be a part of what was consuming everybody's attention and time. I was allowed to attend the meetings with my older sister, Larene, and we usually joined other teenagers from our neighborhood.

I loved going to the meetings because there was always so much emotion and energy. Ministers would be preaching, but not like Sunday preaching when they read scriptures and spoke about things that happened hundreds of years ago when God created the world. This was like "you need to get up and do something about this situation that's happening to you right now" kind of preaching. The songs were in the tune of familiar church hymns and Negro spirituals with words substituted to relate to the movement struggle. We sang them with so much harmony and determination. I just loved them and would stand most of the evening singing my heart out.

The church would always be packed — and hot — and there would be almost as many people on the outside as there were inside. The speakers would get the crowd excited with their recitations of the unequal treatments of Negroes, and then the audience would start singing those freedom songs, which raised the level of emotion even higher.

These meetings were making people aware of just how poor and unequal our living conditions were. We could not eat in restaurants, had to sit upstairs in the movie theater, and had to drink water out water fountains that were designated "For Coloreds." We could only use public restrooms marked "For Coloreds" above the door;

could not use the public libraries; could not use certain public swimming pools; attended segregated public schools and, in some cases, had to walk miles to get to them; were issued outdated, used textbooks while White students received the new editions; lived in segregated communities on many unpaved streets; were buried in segregated cemeteries; had to ride in the back of buses and give up our seats even in the back of the bus if any Whites boarded and needed seats; were hired for menial jobs regardless of our qualifications; and were subject to false arrests with all-White juries determining guilt or innocence. The list went on and on. It was a funny thing, though; we had lived under these conditions all our lives, but for many Negroes, it only began to sink in at these meetings and made us want to change them. We had accepted the existing conditions as our way of life. And in a very sad way, many of us believed we were happy.

There was a lot going on besides the Monday night mass meetings. Strategies were being developed about how to get people registered to vote and educate them on the importance of voting. Movement leaders continued efforts to meet with local officials to present their concerns and reach, without success, some compromises on a few demands. Other actions included successfully boycotting the city transit system; Negroes walked and carpooled instead of riding the city buses. Unsuccessful attempts were made to eat at the lunch counter at the five-and-ten cent store downtown and to receive service at the front window of the popular Arctic Bear, instead of having to order from the side window designated for

Negroes. Several Negro teenagers went to the all-White public swimming pool, so the city closed all public swimming pools, including the one for Negroes, rather than integrate them. There were also unsuccessful attempts to use the downtown public library. And there were several marches where young people, in particular, were arrested.

So the first 6 weeks of my summer vacation were spent being educated about the real world for Negroes. I found out just how depressed life was for us, not only in Albany but all over the South. I wanted to help change things, but I kept that to myself for fear I wouldn't be allowed to attend the meetings if anyone sensed that I might try to do something crazy like "march."

I was learning so much at these meetings. It was a lesson in history as it was unfolding. It was exciting to be among so many people who wanted to help change things, people who put action behind their words. I truly was influenced by the courage of those in the movement.

By mid-July, the weather was heating up and so was the movement. It was announced that Dr. Martin Luther King, Jr., would be in Albany on Saturday, July 21st, and would be at Shiloh that evening for a special mass meeting. I had heard a lot about Dr. King, both on the television news and at some of the mass meetings. He was the head of an organization that helped Negroes peacefully protest against segregationist laws in their fight for racial equality. I later learned that the organization was the Southern Christian Leadership Conference. He had been to Albany a few times before, but I hadn't been at any of the meetings when he was present. Although I had not been to a Saturday meeting before—the meetings were usually held on Monday nights—I knew I had to go to this meeting. I didn't know whether there would be a problem getting permission because the next day was Sunday and that meant being ready to go to Sunday school and church services.

Early that Saturday morning, Larene and I eagerly did our chores, including washing and hanging the family laundry on the clothes lines to dry in the hot July sun, pressing our dresses, and polishing our shoes for Sunday. We didn't want anything standing in our way when it was time to go to the meeting. Although Larene was excited, it did not compare to my anxiousness.

I had decided early in the week that if Dr. King led a march on Saturday evening, as he was now doing in other cities that he visited, I was going to march with him. I felt mature enough to make that decision! To prepare for a possible march that night, I chose to wear a skirt with large front pockets. As Larene and I headed out for the meeting, I put into my skirt pockets a toothbrush; a small amount of toothpaste, from the family tube, on a piece of wax paper; a wash cloth; and a piece of soap that I'd broken off from the only bar of soap that was in our family bathroom.   At 13 years old, I was on my way to a life-changing event, and I hoped I would never be the same afterward.

CHAPTER TWO

I was extremely nervous as we walked the approximate eight blocks to Shiloh Baptist Church. At 6:00 p.m., it was still a hot July evening, and I was sweating more than usual.

Larene said, "Girl, stop walking so fast. It's too hot out here. Besides, we have plenty of time before the meeting starts."

"Sorry," I responded, as I slowed my pace.

Actually, I hadn't realized I was walking so fast. I probably was preoccupied with feelings of guilt because I was planning to do something that I knew would not be acceptable to my parents. I knew better and hadn't been raised to be deceitful and sneaky. Yet, I didn't see any other way because they never would have approved my participating in a march at my young age. There had been too many conversations in our house about the dangers of marching and being arrested. They had seen too much violence across the South in the past year and believed it could happen to marchers in Albany, as well. I had heard all of this, but I knew I had to do it.

There was a big crowd already assembled in front of the church when we arrived, and it was only about 6:30, still 30 minutes before the meeting was to start. We made our way into the sanctuary, which was almost full.

Excitement was already in the air, and people were singing and swaying to the freedom songs. You could barely hear the piano, which desperately needed a tune-up. We found space in the middle of a pew near the back and eased into our seats. I spotted a few of my classmates and other older teenagers in the crowd. Because Carver was the only junior high and Monroe the only high school for Negroes, everyone knew everyone else or their siblings or cousins.

After singing several freedom songs, including "Oh Freedom," Larene's favorite, the speakers came from the pastor's study onto the pulpit to a standing ovation and the thunderous applause from the audience. There were seven or eight men and I couldn't tell which one was Dr. King. I was on my tip-toes but because everyone was standing and the crowd had gotten larger, it was hard to see or hear what was going on. After what seemed like 10 minutes of applause, speakers came forward to report on the status of several concerns that had been brought before Albany's elected officials, about the arrests of several citizens over the past week, what Attorney C. B. King was doing to get them released, and what needed to happen next.

I was shaking almost uncontrollably by now. Larene punched me on my arm and signaled for me to stop squirming so much. I couldn't help it. I was so busy anticipating the moment I would break away from Larene that I didn't even hear them introduce Dr. King. I only remember him speaking at such a fever pitch that no one was sitting, except me, maybe, because my knees were too weak to support me when I tried to stand. I didn't realize until much later in life how paralyzing guilt could be.

Dr. King said that it was time for Negroes in Albany, Georgia, to stop talking about wanting to be free and start doing something about it.

"Tonight is the time to stop talking and start marching. It is time to move."

And with that, he came out of the pulpit and headed down the aisle toward the door. Members of the audience starting falling in line behind him, clapping their hands and singing:

> *Ain't gonna let nobody turn me 'round, turn me 'round, turn me round. Ain't gonna let nobody turn me 'round. I'm gonna keep on a-walking, keep on a-talking, marching up to freedom land.*

> *Ain't gonna let no nervous Nellie turn me 'round, turn me 'round, turn me 'round. Ain't gonna let no nervous Nellie turn me 'round. I'm gonna keep on a-walking, keep on a-talking, marching up to freedom land.*

> *Ain't gonna let Chief Pritchett turn me 'round, turn me 'round, turn me 'round. Ain't gonna let Chief Pritchett turn me 'round. I'm gonna keep on a-walking, keep on a-talking, marching up to freedom land.*

As the long line passed us at the back of the sanctuary, I began easing to the end of our pew. I had a pocketbook that I left on the pew, hoping that Larene would pick it up.

"Noo, what are doing? Get your pocketbook," she said as she sang with the congregation.

I said, "I'm marching," and dashed out of the pew to the end of the line.

I heard her calling my name, but I kept moving with the line.

When I got outside, everyone was lined up in twos. I happened to end up with my classmate and friend, Jackie. I was relieved to be with her. We were next to the last two marchers. It seemed like two or three hundred marchers were ahead of us. I really don't know. No one was talking or singing now, just marching. You only heard the sound of moving feet on the paved sidewalk.

We had marched to Jackson Street, which was about two blocks from the church. Suddenly I felt a yank on my arm that almost scared me to death. It was Larene. She had caught up with us, and when I turned to face her, she had a stern but scared look on her face.

"You'd better get out of that line right now so we can go home," she warned me.

"It's too late for me to get out," I whispered back at her, lifting my hands as if I had surrendered.

She was walking along beside me but a little off the sidewalk, making it obvious that she was not one of the marchers.

"Mama is going to kill you," she said half under her breath.

A few more steps forward and, "You're gonna get me in trouble if I go home without you, Idiot!"

I was sorry I was doing this to her, but there was no turning back for me. The die was cast!

Then suddenly the line stopped moving and we realized that the marchers had begun kneeling. As we knelt, we could hear them praying ahead of us. We were in the Harlem section of town, at Jackson Street and Oglethorpe Boulevard, next to the bus station and across from Jimmie's Hot Dogs. I didn't know what was happening and why we were kneeling and praying.

Then I heard a much louder voice through a megaphone say, "Cease and desist now or you will be placed under arrest."

I was told that it was Chief Pritchett, police chief for the city of Albany, who was talking.

We did not move.

He again ordered that we cease and desist or be arrested.

We still did not move.

In an even louder voice with much more authority he said, "I'm ordering you one last time to cease and desist this unlawful assembly NOW or be placed under arrest."

No one moved.

He then said, "You are all under arrest!"

It was official now. I never looked around for Larene after that.

It seemed that we stayed on our knees a half hour or more after being placed under arrest, and it was extremely uncomfortable being on the pavement in that position. We couldn't hear what was going on at the front of the line where the police officers were, so we followed the actions of the marchers who were in line ahead us. Finally, everyone began standing and moving forward.

We walked at a faster pace now, crossing Broad and Pine Avenues and down an alley where we were led into the back of a large building and into a small room. This was the court house, I later learned. Police officers, all of them White, began ordering us around as they took our names, dates of birth, addresses, and parents' names and their places of employment.

When I gave my name as SavannahBelle Richards, the officer looked at me with contempt and said that he only wanted my first and last names. I nervously told him that I *had* given him my first and last names only. He growled at me, saying that what I gave him constituted three names and shouted for me to give him only what he asked for. So, I conceded, eagerly, that I was Savannah Richards.

Another officer was heard saying to a boy named LC, "Your name is not a couple of initials. What is your first name?"

LC, who ordinarily was outspoken and confident, repeated almost in a whisper, "My name is LC."

"Can you believe this boy?" the officer yelled across the room. "He's standing here swearing that his name is two letters, two alphabets. I bet if I use my billy club across his head, he'll give it to me."

Turning his attention back to LC, he said, "I tell you what, boy, I'm gonna give you a name tonight. Your name is Lucky Charlie. You got it?"

The other officers were roaring with laughter.

With his head bowed, LC answered, "Yes sir."

This "booking" process went on for more than an hour. I was filled with anxiety now because they were collecting information about our parents' employment. My dad worked for the government, at the Marine Base, and if I caused him to lose his job, it would be the end of me, and my family for that matter. My thoughts were racing now because I had not anticipated this possible consequence to my actions. It was hard for me to concentrate, but I knew I had to remain alert.

I estimate that at around midnight, we finally were told that everybody who was 18 and under was to follow several officers down a long hallway and out a door to two waiting buses. The buses appeared to be school buses. We were piled onto the two buses and seated three and four to seats made for two, with the overflow standing in the aisle. Two officers were in the back of the bus with their billy clubs in hand, and the third one was up front with a pistol in his hand. They all seemed to be ready for action.

The buses were filthy and mud appeared to cover the windows, which also had bars on them, making it impossible to see through them. On my bus, the windows were shut tightly and locked, which meant that no air was circulating. I later learned it was the same on the other bus.

It seemed that we sat on the buses in the court house parking lot for about 15 minutes. Everyone was perspiring heavily, probably as much from nervousness as from the heat. I felt nauseous from the gas fumes of the idling bus. Twice, bile came up in my throat but I was able to control it without throwing up, which would have been a disaster because we were packed so closely on the bus.

Without a word from the officers, including the driver, the bus pulled off with a violent jerk. We almost slid off the seats and as we were readjusting, the bus made a sharp turn and those standing fell over on those who were seated. As we were trying to help them, the pistol-drawn officer pointed his gun and shouted, "Stand up!"

Everyone quickly got back in position.

The heat on the bus was unbearable. Willie, one of the older boys, finally asked one of the officers in the back of the bus if a window could be opened so we could get some air. Willie had an air of authority and disgust in his voice; after all, he was going into his senior year of high school. This apparently was unknown to the officer, because he squeezed his way to where Willie was standing midway the bus and cracked him on the head with his billy club.

Almost everyone screamed in fear.

The officer, seemingly with fire in his eyes, turned, looked at all of us, and warned, "The rest of you niggers will get the same or worse if I hear one word from you. Now shut up!"

An already quiet bus became even quieter. Blood was dripping from Willie's head and tears were rolling down his face. Tears began falling from my eyes, too, because now I realized that we all might be killed.

We had been riding about an hour when the bus made two or three turns and came to a sudden stop. The driver turned the motor off. All of us started looking around anxiously. We had no idea where we were or in what direction we had traveled.

We sat for about half an hour before we were ordered to get off the bus. It was dark and I would guess that it was around 1 o'clock in the morning. We were led inside a fenced area and into a huge building. The girls were led in one direction and the boys in another. Three new officers, who had with them two large dogs, joined two of the three officers that were on the bus I was on. Although the other bus was parked next to the one I was on, I didn't know if the marchers had been taken off the bus because it was so dark.

CHAPTER THREE

As we walked, single file, down a long corridor, we could hear chains and keys and doors opening ahead of us. We turned and went down another corridor where I could now see chains being removed and a door opening. F i n a l l y , w e were led into a very large jail cell, with the dogs right at the door nipping at our heels as we passed them. The officers were laughing because we were so frightened of the dogs. The last two girls in line were pushed into the cell, almost falling on their faces, and the door was shut with a loud bang. We could hear the chains being placed back on the door and the dogs barking ferociously.

Lo and behold, as I turned to look at the cell, I saw about 10 girls from Albany already in there! I knew as many of them as I did of the ones who were in my marching group. Some were even my classmates. But the best surprise of all was seeing one of my best friends, Bonnie.

"SavannahBelle," Bonnie screamed. "I don't believe it! Not the scary girl I know."

We hugged each other. Then I said, "Shut your mouth! I am not scary. Anyway, how long have you been here, girl?"

"Since Thursday night, and this place is no picnic. Come on over to my cubicle. There're only two of us in it so far, a girl from Monroe, named Dean, and me."

Bonnie leaned closer and whispered, "Let's pick who else we want before somebody is forced on us, 'cause it's gonna get mighty crowded in here."

Bonnie invited my marching partner, Jackie, and two other classmates, Dee-Dee and Pat, to share the cubicle.

We learned from the other girls that we were in Camilla, which was about 40 miles from Albany. Most of them had been in jail only 2 days, but a couple of them had been in 3 days. In addition to the group of girls who came in with me, there were now 67 girls in the cell. Our ages ranged from 13 to 18 years, 9th grade to recent high school graduates.

Although it was after 1:00 o'clock in the morning, well past my bedtime, I was so tense that I didn't feel at all sleepy or tired. I was trying to see how many of the girls I knew and check out our dismal surroundings. I was shocked at the accommodations.

The cell appeared to be about the length of a basketball court, with 10 small cells or cubicles along one side of the structure. Except for the first cubicle, there were two solid walls where two sets of bunk beds were anchored. The back enclosure had bars from floor to ceiling that allowed us to look out to a spacious corridor where there were big windows across the top of its outer wall, which allowed plenty of light to come into the cell, both during the day and at night, from the street lights. The first cubicle had a solid back wall where a toilet was anchored. All cubicles had bars across their entrance with an opening where a door had once been.

I would guess that each cubicle was probably 8 feet by 8 feet.

In the center of the cell was a long iron picnic-style eating table with benches. In the far back corner, across from the 10th cubicle, was an open bathroom consisting of another toilet, a shower, and a small sink. Neither toilet had a seat. The girls had hung a sheet in front of this area to provide some degree of privacy.

The three solid walls that enclosed the cell were made of cinder block. The longest of those three walls was across the floor from the 10 cubicles and had six small windows with bars high on the wall near the ceiling. We were told that this wall faced the city's main street, but the only way to be able to see outside was to stand on the picnic table or, if you were tall enough, you could stand on one of the benches.

The girls said that the long corridor on the other side of the cubicles with the big windows on the wall was used primarily by the jail trustee, Benny, a fortyish-looking Negro man who would do favors for us if we paid him.

Shocked, I asked Bonnie, "Does anyone in here have money?"

"Nickels and dimes, girl, but they add up."

My first taste of jail reality was when it was time to try to get some sleep. I had not realized that there were no mattresses on the iron bunk beds nor were there enough beds to accommodate all the girls. There were 40 bed frames and 67 girls. This meant that there were 27 more girls than there were beds so almost everyone would have to double up. Some girls chose to sleep atop the picnic table and on the narrow benches rather than squeeze on a bunk bed. The girls who were there when we arrived said we would get used to the discomfort of sleeping on the iron frames.

I didn't go to sleep at all that first night. Bonnie, Jackie, and I sat on Bonnie's bed and talked and giggled the rest of the night. As the morning light began to enter the cell, more chatter could be heard. Girls were still learning who was there and what it had been like for those who had been locked up for a few days.

At about 7 o'clock the next morning, Sunday, we heard the banging of the cell doors and learned from the other girls that they were bringing breakfast. I hadn't thought about food but suddenly realized how hungry I was. After hearing several banging doors, we could hear the jiggling of keys that opened the outer door to our cell and soon the inside cell door was opened.

We were ordered to line up beside the long solid wall. There were two officers and two other men who weren't wearing police uniforms. They pushed two large carts inside the cell door. We were told to take a plate and spoon from the first cart and proceed to the next cart. At the second cart, one of the men served our plates. The menu was cold thick grits with grease-gravy poured over them, fatback, a slice of white bread, and a plastic cup of water that had a cloudy film on top.

I whispered as I headed to a spot at the table, "I can't eat this."

One of the girls who had been there a few days said, "Don't throw it away. Someone else might want it. You'll eat it when you get hungry enough."

I was hungry and knew I would get hungrier, but I couldn't see myself eating that food. No one else wanted my plate.

Lunch was a similar routine of lining up to be served. The menu was peanut butter sandwiches and water. Again, I could not stomach swallowing that.

Dinner was served at 5 o'clock. This was Sunday, so certainly, I thought, we would have a special meal. No such luck! We had fatty, greasy beef stew; potatoes; two slices of white bread; and sweet, syrupy tea. Because the food was cold, the grease was thick and white. Again, I couldn't eat any of it nor drink the sugary tea.

Many of the other girls were also having problems eating the food. Some ate the bread and tried to scrape off the grease and pull the fat off the meat, making every effort to eat some of the disgusting food.

After a day of chattering, dozing off and on, and wondering how long some of us could survive on the jailhouse meals, we decided on Sunday evening to have church service.

We gathered in the center of the cell and began singing spirituals and were really enjoying the harmony. Everybody joined in. Because many of the freedom songs were sung in the tune of spirituals, we easily transitioned into a few of them. Someone started singing "Oh Freedom," and I immediately thought of Larene because she loved this song so much:

> Oh, oh freedom, oh, oh freedom, oh freedom over me, over me.
> And before I'll be a slave, I'll be buried in my grave and go home to my Lord and be free.
>
> No segregation, no segregation, no segregation over me, over me.
> And before I'll be a slave, I'll be buried in my grave, and go home to my Lord and be free.

I almost cried because we sang it so beautifully. Then Brenda, one of the older girls, began to pray spontaneously. I was so amazed at her prayer. I had never heard a teenager pray with the kind of power she had.

"Jesus, O Jesus," she said, "We need you right now, Lord. Yes, we need you and only you. We need you in this jailhouse tonight."

Raising her voice like a preacher, she continued, "We need you to keep the devil away from us. We need you to protect us because our mothers and fathers can't while we are locked up. They don't even know where to find us. We need you to free us from these devils, Lord. There is evil all around us. We don't know how long we will be here but we shall *not* be moved!"

Then someone started singing and the rest of us joined in:

> *We shall not be, we shall not be moved. We shall not
> be, we shall not be move. Just like the tree planted by
> the water, we shall not be moved.*

And some of the girls were shouting "Amen," and "Thank
you, Jesus."

"I wonder what churches they attend," I whispered to
Bonnie.

"Girl, who knows?" she snickered. "They sure don't go to
my little church. Only the deacons pray like that, and ladies
aren't even allowed to pray in church."

"So, God, we beg you to change things for Negroes," Brenda
kept praying. "Don't let White people continue to treat us
like slaves. Let us see some of heaven right here on earth.
Thank you for hearing our prayer. Hallelujah! Hallelujah!
Amen."

Everybody joined in, "Amen, Amen."

As we began returning to our cubicles, many, it seemed,
now filled with what my grandmother may have described
as the Holy Ghost, Brenda said to Diane, one of the other
older girls, "I heard you were talking about me today and I
don't let nobody talk about me. You got something to say,
hussy, then say it to my face!"

"Who do you think you're calling a hussy, hussy? I haven't
said anything about you. Besides, you ain't significant

enough for me to waste my precious time talking about," Diane responded, as she got right in Brenda's face. Diane was about 3 inches taller than Brenda, so she towered over her.

Then the two of them started a nasty exchange of insults and curse words. And it was all about a boy whom Brenda liked. According to some of the girls, he didn't like Brenda but was crazy about Diane.

Some of Diane's friends gathered around her, so Brenda began backing away as she continued uttering less threatening insults.

I couldn't believe my ears! I couldn't believe what had just happened! I'd never experienced such a mood switch before. This was the girl who had just prayed her heart out on our behalf, convincing me she was almost a preacher. In a flash, she had transformed from being a humble angel to an evil devil. She was right; there was evil around us and she was part of the problem. This made me very, very sad.

CHAPTER FOUR

After a restless second night of trying to sleep on an iron bunk bed frame with Bonnie, and with the confrontation between Brenda and Diane playing over and over in my head, it was again time for breakfast.

I had gotten up earlier and brushed my teeth, using just a smidgen of my toothpaste so that it would last, and tried to take a shower. The water was cold and there was no water pressure. The floor of the shower was filthy and had mildew on it. I tried to stand so that only my heels touched the floor; I kept my toes elevated hoping that I would avoid getting athlete's foot between my toes. I smelled funky so I knew I had to endure the discomfort. However, the way it smelled in the cell, in general, it would have been almost impossible for anybody to pinpoint the source of any odor. The smell came in waves, and depending on your frame of mind, you could ignore it or become sick to the stomach. At that moment, I was able to ignore it.

We repeated the routine of lining up against the wall, getting a plate and spoon from the first cart, and being served from the second cart. There was a different man serving the food on this morning. He had a cigar hanging in the side of his mouth, and he used his hand to dip the grits out of the pot onto our plates. Yes, he used his bare, ungloved hand!

This was the nastiest and most disgusting thing I had ever seen! This unshaven, cigar-smoking man put his grubby bare hand in the food that we were to eat! He put the grease-gravy on top of the grits using a rusty spoon. A g a i n, w e had fatback and white sliced bread; this also was handled with his bare hand. However, the water did not have a film over it on this morning.

As much as I hate to admit it, I ate the center of the bread and drank a swallow of the water. I had to have something in my stomach. I felt sick before I ate it and sicker after I ate it. This was certainly a time when I had to control my thoughts about what was going on in order to keep from vomiting.

Soon after breakfast, I had my first sighting of Benny, the jail trustee. He had a push broom, mop, and pail and was beginning to sweep up and down the corridor while keeping his eyes on our cell. The girls who had been in the longest were familiar with him and began talking to him. They were asking if he could bring sodas and other snacks to us from the store because the food we were served was so nasty.

"Sure, gimme me the money," he grinned.

"How do we know you won't keep our money?"

"It looks like y'all will just have to trust me. Anyway, how do you think I became a trustee, baby? They trust me!"

Many of the girls hollered with laughter.

"Tell me this, who got the problem, you or me?" he asked.

"You got a point there, Benny," someone agreed with him.

"I tell you what. I'm going to the store to get some cigarettes befo' lunch and since I'm already going, I won't charge you just this one time. Give me the money for what you want."

The girls put together $3.76 and asked him to bring as many sodas, chips, cookies, and candy as the money would buy.

A girl named Pearl pulled one of the benches under the window to keep an eye out for Benny since the store was on the corner adjacent to the jail.

After a while, she yelled in excitement, "Here he comes, here he comes!"

She said that Benny was coming out of the store with two large paper bags.

The girls who had pooled their money said they would share with all of us. Having abandoned my pocketbook in the church, I was grateful because I didn't have a penny to contribute.

It seemed to be taking Benny a long time to come back with the snacks after Pearl announced that he had come out of the store.

Someone asked, "What if he doesn't bring us anything or doesn't give us our money back?"

About that time, we heard the opening and slamming of doors. It was lunchtime. We repeated the routine of lining up and being served. This time, we had jelly sandwiches and that sweet, syrupy tea.

I ate the edge of one slice of bread and drank a swallow of tea, but it had just too much sugar. I was still extremely hungry and began worrying about how long I would be able to survive on the little food I was eating.

I heard hand clapping and squealing from the girls and turned to see Benny out in the corridor with two large paper bags. He was sweating. He told us to hurry and take the items and hide them, as he handed them through the bars. He said he almost got caught because it was hard to hide two big bags.

We all thanked him over and over. He had bought 20 sodas, several bags of chips, cookies, and candy bars. We all shared the goodies. I had a cookie and a penny candy bar, and shared a bag of chips and soda with, Bonnie, Dee-Dee, and Jackie. I thought it was the best tasting food I had had in my whole life!

Later that afternoon, after we nibbled on our snacks, we heard some commotion outside. Pearl and another girl named Marie jumped on the benches and looked out the window. Pearl reported that there was a city of Albany garbage truck in front of the jail.

'Oh no," she screamed!

"What? What?" several girls asked as they scrambled to get a spot on one of the benches to take a look.

"Girls, the boys are being led to the truck by several guards and big dogs," Marie said anxiously.

"What's happening? Oh, Lord, are they loading them in the truck to crush them and take them to the dump to bury them?" screamed one girl in anguish.

"Hold on, hold on! Well, will you look at this! The garbage truck is loaded with mattresses. They're using the boys to unload it," Pearl explained in a relieved voice.

Almost immediately, we could hear the banging of the jail doors in the distance. We all scrambled to make sure we were presentable. Then we heard the jiggling of keys as the door to our cell was soon opened. And there they were, our boys! Their backs were slightly bent as they brought the mattresses in under the direction of the guards and eyes of three large dogs.

Some of the boys were going with some of the girls and they were trying to sneak kisses or hugs as they placed the mattresses on the frames. I was shocked to see Steven, a rising junior whom I had a huge crush on. I didn't even know he was in jail! Apparently, he had marched at an earlier rally. He was so cute and popular! He had no idea I was in love with him. Only Bonnie knew that and I had given her the eye to keep her mouth closed.

Steven's girlfriend, Nona, was also in jail. They were seen sneaking a kiss when he took a mattress to one of the back cubicles.

"Boy, oh boy, how lucky can you be?" Jackie asked, almost to herself.

After all of the mattresses were in place and the boys and guards had left, many of the girls started jumping up and down with joy because they had seen their boyfriends. The rest of us jumped up and down because we had something soft we could sleep on. Even though the mattresses were dirty and musty smelling, we were jubilant because our bodies ached from sleeping and sitting on metal.

As I sat on the mattress relaxing, I decided to start writing about what was happening to us during our stay in jail. I didn't have any paper but, to get started, I improvised by using one of the large paper bags Benny brought our snacks in. What "back-to- school essays" we would be able to write when we returned in September! This was like no other summer I'd ever had.

I was snapped back to reality when I heard commotion in the back of the cell.

"You bumpy face sapsucker, with your short hair-r-r! You been pickin' on me all day, now I'm ready for you," cried a girl with a thick Southern drawl.

I jumped off my bunk bed to find out what was going on. Most of the girls were gathering outside their cubicles into the open area of the cell. My 13-year-old classmate, Flora, was livid! She was hyperventilating and had started pacing and shouting to the top of her lungs at a girl named Quin, a recent high school graduate.

"You been strutting 'round in my housecoat for 3 days! I haven't had a chance to wear it none! And you took my hair rollers and comb. I don't want any of my stuff back now. I'm just sick of you! You, you old outhouse smelling, mildew lips, pancake chest, alley cat," Flora continued shouting.

Quin didn't respond as she stood in the center of the cell looking shocked and embarrassed.

Flora's sudden and unusual outburst shocked everybody. She was quiet, cute, and well liked. It was obvious, though, that she had taken all she planned to take.

One of the older girls pulled Flora to the side to calm and comfort her.

Quin was wearing a housecoat that seemed too little for her, and her hair was in rollers.

Bonnie whispered to me, "I'm no lawyer, but looks like the evidence speaks for itself. Quin is rather sneaky and spooky acting. I think she took advantage of Flora because of her age. Hey, but Flo showed her!"

Quin slithered back into her cubicle, speechless, so it seemed there would be no fight or any additional excitement at this time. The other girls wandered back to their cubicles.

Once Bonnie, Jackie, Dee-Dee, Pat, and I got back to our cubicle, we buried our faces in the musty-smelling mattresses to smother our hysteria.

"You bumpy face sapsucker, with your short hair-r-r," snickered Bonnie.

We were going crazy trying to smother and control our laughter.

"No, no," I said, "The funniest part was when she said, 'You outhouse smelling, mildew lips, pancake chest, alley cat.'"

"Oh, Lord, save me," Jackie screamed with laughter as she buried her head in the mattress.

Then, it became overwhelming and we just couldn't help it. Our laughter escaped our mouths and could be heard throughout the cell. This was the funniest verbal attack we had ever heard.

Pat had climbed on the top bunk bed and was kicking her legs in the air, laughing so hard that she was breathless. Dee-Dee, on a lower bed, pounded her fists into the mattress, hollering as she laughed.

I laughed so much that my stomach cramped. We continued laughing uncontrollably, between whispered recitations of Flora's attack, for what must have been 15 minutes. We just couldn't control ourselves.

Finally, Quin walked to the opening of our cubicle and shouted, "Shut the crap up!"

That brought about even harder and louder laughter because she still was wearing Flora's housecoat and her hair was in those pink rollers that also belonged to Flora. And, she had a bumpy face. She glared at us angrily and then suddenly stormed away.

Jackie was now on her knees hollering with laughter, out of control. And our laughter was contagious, because soon laughter could be heard coming from other cubicles.

If I had been alone, I would have been afraid of Quin; but I was surrounded by friends and Quin was on the defensive, so my laughter grew even louder. And no matter how hard I tried, I could not stop laughing.

Then an older girl named Trudy, who wanted to appear more mature and sensible than most of the girls, and she probably was, stood on top of the eating table to get everyone's attention and asked that we all bow our heads and pray. Of course, that quieted everyone. After all, we were in jail for religious-based, Constitutional-entitlement reasons.

Trudy prayed a long and softly spoken prayer.

She said, "Lord, come by our cell and keep us in harmony. We need you to guide us because we are children. When we do something wrong, we need forgiveness. We know that you don't have time for fussing and fighting. We are looking for freedom. Petty things need to be left on the playground. Silly things have no place in the fight for freedom. We need to be serious. If we can't be serious, we need to go home."

"I know she's talking about us being silly, but we didn't start any of this," Bonnie said to me under her breath.

Shh," I said, "We did get out of hand."

Trudy's prayer seemed to settle everybody down. To put the icing on the cake, a couple of the girls began softly singing, and everybody joined in:

> *Come by here, My Lord, come by here.*
> *Come by here, My Lord, come by here, Oh Lord.*
> *Come by here, My Lord, come by here. Oh*
> *Lord, come by here.*
>
> *Somebody needs you, Lord, come by here.*
> *Somebody needs you, Lord, come by here, Oh*
> *Lord. Somebody needs you, Lord, come by here,*
> *Oh Lord, come by here.*
>
> *Singing and praying, Lord, come by here.*
> *Singing and praying, Lord, come by here, Oh Lord.*
> *Singing and praying, Lord, come by here, Oh Lord,*
> *come by here.*

In the calmness and quietness of the evening, with mattresses that helped to soothe our weary bodies, I began thinking about how one of my grandmothers always said how much we really need the Lord.

CHAPTER FIVE

My mind drifted back to an incident three summers earlier when I was 10 years old and visiting my grandmother in Cuthbert, a small town in South Georgia. Grand Vann is what we called Grandmother Savannah. I always loved spending time at her house during the summer because I felt independent and grown-up. Grand Vann lived on the main Negro street in Cuthbert, so everything worth knowing or worth seeing happened on Andrew Street. We could sit on her huge front poach and catch it all. Grand Vann also lived adjacent to a café, or juke joint as she sometimes called it. There was plenty of music and laughter every Friday and Saturday night.

I would sit near the end of the porch, which was closest to the café, so I could hear the laughter, especially from the ladies. There were different sounds to their laughter. Some were raspy, some were breathless and high pitched, and my favorite one had a lingering growl that seemed to snap at you. It was such a sweet sound. I never saw their faces or knew who was doing the laughing, but I imagined they were having the time of their lives, dancing and smoking cigarettes, sitting on café stools. I dreamed of being one of those ladies, with a beautiful laugh, having fun in a café.

Grand Vann didn't know I had such aspirations. She would have quickly dispelled such outrageous thoughts. She just enjoyed having me sit with her as we watched the people entertain themselves. We would sit on her front porch from late afternoon, right after dinner, until about 9:30 p.m. I would have to take my bath and put on my pajamas at 8 but I was allowed to stay on the porch with her until she was ready to prepare for bed at 9:30.

People who had cars would ride up and down Andrew Street while others walked. Age didn't matter. Everybody was out on weekends.

This particular late July Friday night seemed to have so much excitement in the air. People were laughing and talking as they strolled up and down the street and, as usual, speaking to Grand Vann as they passed her house. It seemed like a big street party, so when 9:30 rolled around, I didn't want to go to bed and begged to stay up a little longer. Grand Vann agreed and we sat until a little past 10 o'clock. I was fast asleep as soon as my head hit the pillow.

The clanging of empty beer bottles being dumped into a metal barrel woke me on Saturday morning, and I quickly rose, leaning on my elbows, to begin counting. I pushed the curtains aside so I could feel the breeze that was coming through the open window. It was just after 7 o'clock in the morning. A second dumping made a more thunderous sound. While I couldn't see the barrel, I could smell the stale beer odor from across the narrow side street that separated Grand Vann's house from the café. A minute later, I heard a third clanging sound of broken glass.

"Oh yes," I whispered, "Keep them coming."

Po-Boy dumped a total of six of those huge buckets into the barrel that morning. I was jubilant as I jumped out of bed. This meant that Mr. Boot, the café owner, would give big scoops of ice cream to the kids that day, maybe even two scoops. I had long ago determined that you could tell whether Mr. Boot had a great Friday night or just an average one by the number of buckets of empty beer bottles that were dumped on Saturday morning. If Po-Boy dumped four or fewer buckets of beer bottles, it was a lousy night even if I had heard the piccolo playing into the wee hours of the morning. However, five or more buckets of empty bottles meant the night had been jumping and Mr. Boot would be in a good mood. Although I was only 10 years old, I was very calculating.

I had my nickel ready and couldn't wait until 5:00 o'clock when Grand Vann would allow me to walk (I actually skipped) over to the café and get an ice cream cone. Kids could enter the café until about dusk; after that, it was grown folk only.

On that Saturday evening, the town's men had gathered at the café for their annual rattlesnake roundup. On Friday and Saturday, they participated in the hunt and brought their prized dead snakes to lay out in front of the café for the judging ritual. The man with the biggest snake would have bragging rights until the next year and would get free beer all evening.

Two of the men were in stiff competition — their snakes were longer than 10 feet. One of them, Mr. Jimmy, was a bit louder than the other men in expressing his excitement to win although they all were yelling and bragging about their kill. Grand Vann said it was nothing unusual, but the police happened to be riding by just at that time.

The two burly White police officers stopped their car in the middle of the street, but no one noticed them because they were focused on the dead snakes. The policemen left their car, without turning it off, in the middle of the street; they walked up behind the crowd of 30 or 40 men. They shined their flashlights at the men, which caught their attention. Within seconds, you could hear a pin drop.

One of policemen asked, "What you boys think you doin', disturbing the peace?"

Nobody said anything.

They continued shining their flashlights in the men's faces, pushing them aside as they made their way to the steps of the café.

Looking at Mr. Jimmy, one of the officers asked, "Boy, didn't you hear me?"

"Yes sir," he responded.

"Is this your snake, boy?"

"Yes sir."

He then made Mr. Jimmy lie down on his stomach on the concrete with his face pressed into the snake. He pulled out his billy club as the other officer put his foot on Mr. Jimmy's back while telling him and the other men that they would not tolerate disorderly conduct in their town, not even in the colored section.

The piccolo had stopped playing and no one was laughing or talking.

Grand Vann said they were making an example of Mr. Jimmy.

He lay on the ground with his face pressed into that snake and the police officer's foot on his back for a long time. When the officer finally removed his foot from Mr. Jimmy's back, the other one hit him hard across his head with the billy club. We were told that blood splattered on those standing near him as Mr. Jimmy cried out in pain. The other men groaned in horror, as did Grand Vann, covering her mouth to quiet her anguish while she prayed, "Come by here, Lord, please come by here. Lord, we need you right now, right here."

Walking backward, the officers slowly returned to their car, as if daring the men to say or do anything, and drove away.

Some of the ladies rushed out of the café and began wrapping Mr. Jimmy's head in towels to stop the bleeding. Then, some of the men carried him home.

Mr. Boot didn't announce a winner of the snake contest for that year. In fact, people turned in early that evening and he closed the café before 10 o'clock.

Grand Vann said any confrontation between Negroes and the law always made her think about poor Lena Baker, a Negro woman in Cuthbert who killed a White man.

She said, "Although it was about 15 years ago, it is still fresh in my mind. I knew Lena and her family; they didn't live far from here, over on the corner of Cherry and Second Street, across from Miss Fluellen's store. She worked for Mr. Knight, who owned a mill near downtown, and there had been whispers that he would keep her locked up at the mill many nights against her will. Although she had children and needed to go home, he wouldn't let her. I guess he thought, like a lot of White folk, that he owned her.

"But one night when he wouldn't let her leave, she fought back. He was going to beat her with a metal pipe, she said, but she grabbed his gun and shot and killed him. She said it was in self-defense, that he would have killed her if she hadn't protected herself. The law saw it differently and said she murdered him in cold blood, and the jury of all White men agreed. She went to the electric chair in a matter of months. We saw firsthand just how the justice system works for Negroes. They talk about swift justice; that had to be a record for the electric chair.

"I get sad every time I think of the day Lena was executed," she continued, seemingly to herself. "Perkins Funeral Home had to go all the way to Reidsville Prison to pick up her body. Mr. Perkins said he arrived at the prison and was standing next to the hearse waiting to be directed to come in to get the body when Lena got his attention from the prison window. He said he nearly fainted because he expected her to already be dead or at least to be strapped in the electric chair. She beckoned for him and, reluctantly, he walked closer to the building. She dropped a note from the window and asked him to give it to her three children. He said he could barely control himself emotionally. Unable to speak, he said he just nodded his head as he picked up the note from the ground."

"Did he give the note to her children?" I asked.

"He said it was the hardest thing he'd ever had to do. The second hardest was bringing her body back to Cuthbert. So tonight, Lord have mercy, when those police officers beat Jimmy, I know nobody out there considered reporting it because who would believe the police did anything wrong? Besides, who would they report it to? 'They were just enforcing the law' would be the response, if they even bothered to say anything at all."

After a brief silence, she said, "Let's get some sleep; tomorrow is Sunday."

I barely slept that night. I was haunted by thoughts of Mr. Jimmy being beaten and Lena Baker dying in that electric chair.

After getting dressed on Sunday morning, I kept waiting for kids to walk by the house as they always did on their way to Sunday school at Payne Chapel AME Church so I could join them for the three-block walk. I didn't see anyone. It was getting late and I was afraid to walk alone for two reasons. I didn't want to walk where those huge snakes had been laid across the sidewalk, and I also didn't want to step on any blood left from Mr. Jimmy's injury. The thought of the beating and all that blood made me tremble with fear.

Grand Vann's house, the café, and the church were on the same side of the street, so I decided I would zigzag to avoid walking in front of the café. I crossed the street in front of Grand Vann's house, ran the first block without looking in the direction of the café, then crossed back and walked the last two blocks to the church. I did the same thing on my return after the church service, even though Grand Vann was now with me and said there was nothing to fear. Other kids also were walking with us. But the image in my head wouldn't let me get close to the café. In fact, I never again walked on the sidewalk in front of the café and never ate another ice cream cone from there.

Someone told Grand Vann on the following Monday that Mr. Jimmy had to be taken for medical treatment because his head was swollen so badly.

Although I returned to Albany by the middle of August, we called Grand Vann once a week and I always asked her how Mr. Jimmy was doing.

"He's about the same, poor man," she would say.

"What does that mean?" I'd ask.

"He's not able to walk steady and is having problems speaking clearly. It's like he's had a stroke."

When Grand Vann visited us at Thanksgiving, she told us that Mr. Jimmy was paralyzed and that he would never be able to care for himself again. He was now living with his sister and her family over in Alabama.

Throughout the Thanksgiving weekend, Grand Vann kept saying how much we need the Lord.

CHAPTER SIX

We still needed the Lord on Tuesday morning in the Camilla jail. As we were getting "dressed" before they brought in breakfast, Benny came on the corridor with his bucket and mop and made an announcement that took me, and others, too, I guessed, by total surprise.

"Well, little ladies," he began, with his chest stuck out, "I guess y'all have smiles on your little faces 'cause today is visitation day."

"Did you say visitation day?" someone yelled over everybody.

"That's right, so y'all better be real good."

It had never occurred to me that we could or may have visitors. What news that was to ponder!

I didn't know if my parents even knew where I was. I was sure they were upset at me. Even if they knew where I was, how would they know today was visitation day? And my dad worked during the week so he certainly couldn't come. Then panic washed over my body as I thought about the possibility that he could have been fired from his job because of me. And if he hadn't been fired and was at work, my mother wouldn't have a way to travel to Camilla. I was becoming distraught.

Of course, I had on the same clothes I had worn on Saturday evening to the mass meeting. I had washed my underwear but not my blouse and skirt. I couldn't help but wonder what they would think of how I looked?

There was no mirror, so I had no idea how my hair looked after Bonnie plaited it. At 13, I was a bit old to be in plaits, but that was the best option to keep my hair from sticking straight up on top of my head.

We went through the breakfast and lunch routines as usual. However, our lunch menu was upgraded to pork and beans and vienna sausages. I surprised myself by eating the three little sausages. They were so good! Nobody was giving away their lunch on this day.

There was so much chatter and everyone was smiling. It was a great day!

About an hour after lunch, Pearl, who seemingly was always on watch, yelled that a large group of Negroes were walking across the street toward the jail, and they were carrying bags and boxes. Everybody started dragging the benches under the windows and climbing on them to try and see if they recognized any of the people. It was chaotic!

Girls were yelling as they recognized their family members and others. I stood on a bench for a couple of minutes but didn't see anyone from my family. There had to be more than a hundred people out there and it was difficult to see everyone.

Many police officers had lined up on the outside of the fence that surrounded the jail. We could see 15 of them.

To my surprise, our visitors were not allowed beyond the outer fence. I had envisioned that we would be brought to a visitor's room to meet with our family members, like they do on television. To the contrary, our visitors had to yell through the fence to voices inside the jail, because they couldn't see us from the distance they were forced to stand. It was difficult to hear because so many of the girls were trying, all at once, to make contact with the visitors.

Finally, everyone realized that we needed some organization, so one of the visitors began calling out the names. As a girl's name was called, she would climb on the bench if she wasn't already there and have a loud conversation with her visitors.

After almost half an hour, my name was called. I wasn't standing on the bench and didn't hear it, so several girls yelled, "SavannahBelle, SavannahBelle, they called your name, girl!"

I ran and jumped on the bench, anxiously looking over the crowd to spot my visitors. Then I saw them! My mother and Larene stood at the fence. I was ecstatic! They had found me!

"Hey, Mama! Hey, Larene!" I thought I shouted, but the girls were telling me to speak up so they could hear me.

"Mama, Larene, can y'all hear me?"

"Are you all right?" Mama shouted back.

"I'm fine," I said, but without the conviction I wanted to express.

"Everybody's been so worried about you, and we've seen so much in the news. Your grandparents and all of us have been praying so hard for you and all the children. I brought you some food and clothes, and some money so you can buy some snacks. They said you could have those things. We're making arrangements to get you out by tomorrow if they'll process the papers. We just found out where you were late yesterday."

"No, no, Mama, I don't want to get out. Everybody is gonna stay in. It's not so bad in here once you get used to it. I know everybody. A lot of the girls are my classmates and some of Larene's, too. There're 67 of us. We want to stay together as a team. I really want to stay. Please, please, let me, Mama," I begged.

"We'll have to see what your dad says this evening."

"Okay," I said, and, suddenly I was overcome with emotion. I wanted to thank her and Larene for coming but couldn't get the words out as I dropped to my knees in sobs. I don't know what brought that about, but I couldn't utter another word.

Bonnie jumped on the bench and shouted, "Hi, Mrs. Richards, this is Bonnie. These girls are pushing to get a chance to talk and SavannahBelle lost her spot on the bench. She's so happy y'all came. Me, too!"

Bonnie didn't want my mother to know I was crying. She would have assumed the worst and worried that I was not doing well. If she thought that, she would certainly get me out.

Everybody got a turn to shout to their visitors before they were told by the guards that they had to leave. I estimated that they had been allowed to stand outside about 2 hours.

I squeezed back on the bench, much more composed than I had been half an hour earlier, and shouted goodbye to my mother and Larene. They had gotten a ride with one of our neighbors, whose son was also in jail.

At around 4:00 o'clock, Benny brought our bags and boxes into our cell. I had a nice size box that contained several items: shorts, blouses, underwear, Mum deodorant, toothpaste, soap, saltine crackers, cans of vienna sausages, peaches, chunks of watermelon wrapped in wax paper, and several ham sandwiches. Mama had also put a *JET* magazine and a small Bible in the box, and had marked several scriptures. There was no money, however. Word got around that Benny had kept the money.

I was so happy to get my box. Not all the girls had visitors or received packages, so I felt real special, particularly since I had disobeyed my parents. And because I was having difficulty eating, I especially appreciated the food.

I shared my ham sandwiches with Bonnie, Jackie, Pat, Dee-Dee, and Dean, my cubicle mates, and with as many others as I could. They were delicious! I saved one for Bonnie and me for later that night. However, I didn't share my watermelon with anybody! I was saving it for the next day.

We were enjoying our sandwiches when Pearl, who was
again looking out the window, shouted, "Hey, look who's
here! Y'all won't believe your eyes, girls. The one and only,
the Rev. Dr. Martin Luther King, Jr., is approaching the
fence with a whole lot of people following him."

The girls jumped up and began climbing on the benches to
get a look. They were screaming and having fits.

"Dr. King, Dr. King, over here," they were yelling.

I hurried over to the benches, too, and we all joined in the
excitement, even though we couldn't all see what was going
on. Some of the girls were pushing to get a space on a bench.

I stood back and in a very mature voice said, "I can wait
until some of you calm down before trying to get a spot on a
bench. After all, those of us who marched last Saturday
night have already seen Dr. King. He led our march!"

Girls turned around looking at me in disbelief.

"Honey, what planet have you been on?" one of them said
mockingly.

Others, mostly those who marched on Saturday night, were
asking, "What are you talking about?"

"Did you say Dr. King led the march? Where did you get
that from?" Trudy asked with some authority.

No one gave me a chance to respond. They fired one
comment after another my way.

"Girl, Dr. King wasn't even in Albany on Saturday night. Rev. Wells, a preacher who's active with the movement, led our march on Saturday night."

"You actually thought you had marched behind the Rev. Dr. Martin Luther King, Jr.? Did you really? This is too funny," Quin poked fun, eager to get back at me for laughing at her during Flora's attack on her.

"Rev. Wells doesn't look anything like Dr. King. Haven't you ever seen Dr. King? He is the most famous Negro this country has ever seen. How could you confuse Rev. Wells with Dr. King?" Videl, one of the older girls asked.

Then Trudy said sarcastically, "Somebody — anybody — give this girl space on a bench right away. She needs to be educated right now."

All of this was said amidst laughter and looks of pity. Even so, I could not let my embarrassment stand in the way of my seeing Dr. King. I climbed on the bench directly in front of where he stood at the fence.

"Wow! Dr. Martin Luther King, Jr. I can't believe I'm seeing him in person. My hero! Oh, my goodness, he looks so young," I found myself saying.

Although I was disappointed to learn that I hadn't marched with Dr. King, I was thrilled that he had come to see us in jail. This was a miracle! The other girls recognized the Rev. Ralph Abernathy as one of the men with Dr. King. They were accompanied by a group of about 30 people, many of them from the Albany movement, including the movement president, Dr. William Anderson.

Dr. King, holding a megaphone in his hand, asked us how we were doing. Everybody, including the boys upstairs, shouted out, "Fine, Dr. King, just fine!"

He said he was very proud of us and encouraged us to stay strong. He also told us that with our help, the jails in Albany and the surrounding towns, like Camilla, were crowded and that the national news had picked up the story.

"Progress is being made on many fronts," he continued.

Dr. King said he wanted to pray for us and the group all kneeled at the fence. It became completely quiet.

I was in such a state of awe that I don't remember much of his prayer. I know he asked God to protect the children and to keep us strong while we were on the battlefield fighting for freedom.

I felt electricity running through my body. When he finished praying, we began cheering and screaming for about 5 minutes. Everybody was celebrating.

Dr. King got back on the megaphone and told us that they had brought boxes of supplies for us and that they were being delivered by the guards. He then said goodbye.

That one visit did more for me than even I could have imagined. Dr. King had motivated me so much that I could have stayed in jail fighting for freedom forever! I was on fire! The whole jail was on fire! We started singing freedom songs and using whatever we could get our hands on to bang on the bars. We also could hear the boys singing and yelling in celebration upstairs. It was history in the making, all because of the great Rev. Dr. Martin Luther King, Jr.

We were singing our hearts out:

> *I woke up this morning with my mind stayed on freedom.*
> *I woke up this morning with my mind stayed on freedom.*
> *I woke up this morning with my mind stayed on freedom.*
> *Hallelu . . . Hallelu . . . Hallelujah.*
>
> *Walking and talking with my mind stayed on freedom.*
> *Walking and talking with my mind stayed on freedom.*
> *Walking and talking with my mind stayed on freedom.*
> *Hallelu . . . Hallelu . . . Hallelujah.*
>
> *It ain't no harm to keep your mind stayed on freedom.*
> *It ain't no harm to keep your mind stayed on freedom.*
> *It ain't no harm to keep your mind stayed on freedom.*
> *Hallelu . . . Hallelu . . . Hallelujah.*

It went on and on. The girls paused a while just to listen to and enjoy the boys stomp and scream. It was pandemonium! The "King" had come!

We paused only to get dinner, which we didn't want, but we also didn't want to take the chance that the guards might stop bringing us meals; we knew that the food our families had brought us wouldn't last very long. Dinner consisted of gooey rice, chicken necks and gizzards, over-cooked English peas, slices of white bread, and cherry punch that wasn't too sweet. Some of the girls ate the meal, but most did not. I drank the punch but didn't eat, nor did any of the girls in my cubicle. I was thinking about the ham sandwich I had saved for Bonnie and me for later that night.

After dinner, we started singing again. We were so happy about the unexpected and extraordinary visitation day and actually having been in the presence of Dr. Martin Luther King, Jr., who personally thanked us and prayed for us. What a marvelous day!

In between our jubilation, we heard banging upstairs. We stopped to listen and then heard one of the boys yell for us to send them some snacks.

Pearl yelled back, "How can we send you snacks? Do you want us to ask Benny to deliver them to you when he comes in tomorrow?"

"Just keep your eyes on the windows," we were told.

We all stared at the windows, wondering what he meant. All of a sudden, we saw something dropping in front of the windows. It was dangling back and forth, a few feet away from the windows.

"What in the world is that?" Pearl asked.

"I don't know, but it looks like cloth tied to . . . oh my goodness; it's their belts tied together to make a rope," one of the other girls who was standing on the benches explained with excitement.

"Can you reach it?" we heard a boy yell.

Etta, one of the taller girls, stuck her arm through the bars and reached out to try and grab the object, but it kept swinging outward.

"Try to hold it steady," she yelled up to the boys.

She kept reaching out and finally was able to grab it. She pulled it in and we saw that the cloth was a shirt. She untied the shirt and asked another girl to hold on to the belts on our end; the boys were holding on upstairs.

The shirt served as a container for the food, and we piled it full of snacks. I gave almost half of what I had. Everybody was generous. In fact, we were so generous that the shirt couldn't get through the bars. We took some of the items out, retied the shirt, and attached it to the belts. Then, we carefully pushed it through the bars. We yelled for them to pull it back up and it began its journey back upstairs.

After a couple of minutes, we heard shouts of, "Mission accomplished! Thank you! We love all y'all!"

We were thrilled that everything had been so perfect on this day.

After things quieted down for the evening, I decided I would take a look at some of the scriptures Mama had marked in the Bible. I was not surprised she chose the 23rd Psalm. Everybody had to memorize the 23rd Psalm, and we often recited it during devotion at school. I found several other scriptures very encouraging and read them over and over:

The Lord is my light and my salvation; whom shall I fear?
The Lord is the strength of my life; of whom shall I be afraid?
(Psalm 27:1)

For in the time of trouble he shall hide me in his pavilion; in the secret of his tabernacle shall he hide me; he shall set me up upon a rock. (Psalm 27:5)

For his anger endureth but a moment; in his favour is life: weeping may endure for a night, but joy cometh in the morning. (Psalm 30:5)

I will lift up mine eyes unto the hills, from whence cometh my help. My help cometh from the Lord, which made heaven and earth. (Psalm 121:1–2)

Judging from the scriptures she chose, Mama seemed to want me to stay strong and feel safe.

CHAPTER SEVEN

I was emotionally drained when I awoke on Wednesday morning. Everyone was still smiling, almost floating on air, when we lined up for breakfast. We had food that our families had brought, had found a way to share what we had with the boys, and had supplies and toiletries from Dr. King and his group. So we were not worried about anything on this morning. I don't even remember what they served us for breakfast.

It was relatively quiet the rest of the morning, and I took advantage of this time to write, while everything was still fresh in my mind, about what we experienced on Tuesday. I was filling up the space on those two paper bags pretty fast and feeling great about all I was capturing.

Belinda, one of the recent high school graduates, came over to me and asked if I'd like to help her with a project. She said she had observed me writing a lot and thought it was a good idea to take notes. She said she had been the editor of Monroe's yearbook staff and had thought about interviewing some of the girls for an article.

"I love your idea! I'll help with whatever you want me to do," I said enthusiastically. I was so excited about her idea and about being a part of such an undertaking.

"Great. I'm thinking about asking them why they marched and what they expect to happen as a result of this experience in jail, something along those lines. Let's get started after lunch," she said.

I couldn't believe it was lunchtime already. To everyone's surprise, they served bologna and cheese sandwiches, cookies, and punch. This was definitely a step up. However, I gave the sandwich to one of the girls and only ate the cookie and drank the punch.

As soon as lunch was over, Belinda announced that she was writing an article and had asked me to assist her in interviewing anybody who wanted to participate in sharing why they had marched. She told everybody that she hoped she would get the article published in *The Southwest Georgian,* our local Negro newspaper. She continued, "I know *The Albany Herald* would never publish it."

One of the girls said, "You know they devote a whole page on Saturdays to Negroes, called News of the Colored People of Southwest Georgia, so you may try to get it in there."

"I think I'll stick with *The Southwest Georgian.* Besides, all I've ever seen in *The Albany Herald* on that page for us is society news like wedding, church, and civic club announcements. I don't think they would print anything we write about civil rights and our jail experience. They only write what they want us to know about such subjects.

"Anyway, I believe our experience behind bars and what motivated us to march would be of interest to other students and even adults. Who knows, our story could move from a small Negro newspaper to the movie theater, so let's keep it interesting."

"Don't you think you're kidding yourself and have your head in the clouds—the movie theater?" one girl in the back laughed.

That comment didn't faze Belinda. She told everyone this would be done on a voluntary basis and if they didn't want to be interviewed, they didn't have to participate. She also said that no names would be used.

"Well, what's the purpose if you're not gonna use our names and give us credit?" another asked.

"Let's get started," she said, ignoring that last question.

A lot of the girls were anxious to be interviewed. I sat at the eating table next to Belinda, feeling important, as she set up to begin the interviews. She gave me several sheets of paper that may have come from a small notepad and said we both could record the interviews and compare notes later.

The first girl to be interviewed was a 16-year-old 11th grader named Rebecca who was rough around the edges and didn't bite her tongue for anybody. In an emphatic tone she said, "I marched so I don't have to pick cotton this summer, and I intend to march as many times as it takes and stay in jail as long as I can. And I'll be moving to New York City as soon as my aunt can afford a bigger apartment and sends for me."

"Yeah, sure," Bonnie whispered, amused, as she had eased in the space next to me at the table.

I ignored her comment and kept writing.

Next was Betty, a 15-year-old 10th grader. She said that she had spent only one night away from home her whole life and that was when she and her mother went to her aunt's house in Tifton 3 years earlier. She said she had marched because she imagined being in jail was like being at camp. She didn't mind that the accommodations were lousy and that she couldn't stomach the food. She was in another town and her mother wasn't there to tell her what to do every minute.

"It's a dream come true!" she yelled.

There were a lot of chuckles after that outburst.

Belinda then interviewed another 16-year-old 11th grader, Martha, whose claim to fame, I learned, was predicting, after the fact, that a certain event would take place and how she had told someone it would occur. She could never say who she'd talked to about her prediction, but she'd swear that she had made the prediction. She, of course, had predicted that the jails would be filled to capacity in every town and she had come to witness it firsthand.

"She's just repeating what Dr. King told us," Bonnie said out the corner of her mouth.

Videl, a 17-year-old intellectual high school graduate, who was preparing to go to college, said, "I participated in the movement because I want to be a part of history, a history that brings about an awareness of the rights of Negroes and a change in the way Negroes are treated as they try to claim those rights. I hope that better job opportunities become available and job training will be offered for people who don't have a skill."

"Very intellectual," Bonnie commented.

Etta, a tall 16-year-old junior who played sports and was a star on the girls' basketball team, said, "I participated 'cause I wanted the opportunity to tell these southern White folks that I ain't afraid of them. They can turn the water hoses on me, put the dogs on me, spit on me, drag me, and insult me. I still won't back down. This is the third time I've marched and the second time I've been arrested. I still ain't through."

"Wow," I heard several of the girls say.

A feisty 13-year-old 9th grader, Kate, another classmate, said, "I marched because I'm not afraid and because I followed my 16-year-old boyfriend. He had just marched 2 weeks ago, but we decided to march together this time so we can tell our children what we went through together."

"Unbelievable," Bonnie whispered. I still ignored her.

A 14-year-old 10th grader named Jessa said she had to get away for a while, because she was tired of babysitting her five younger sisters and brothers. She said this was her first vacation ever.

I had to laugh aloud because that was pretty shrewd.

Mollie, a 14-year–old 10th grader, said she wanted something exciting to write about in her English composition class, because every year, she wrote the same thing about her summer vacation: "I visited my grandparents on their farm, milked the cows, fed the hogs, and ran from the rooster. This year, I want to blow their minds."

Bonnie said, close to my ear, "I like her creative thinking and planning, but what a price to pay just for an English paper." I elbowed her.

Sixteen-year-old 11th grade twins, May and Kay, along with their 15- and 13-year-old sisters, Karen and Kitty, were in jail together. Their brother also was in jail upstairs. They were from a family of nine children and said their mother had told all the older kids to march and stay in jail as long as they would keep them so she could have some peace and quiet and save on their grocery expenses!

"Just kidding," one of the twins said.

Bonnie mumbled, "Did anybody see their mama visiting them yesterday?"

"Shut up," I said under my breath.

Another 11th grader, Esther, who said she was 16 but was rumored to be 17 or 18, was tough and nobody bothered her.

She looked Belinda in the eye and said in a slow, throaty voice, "It ain't nobody's doggone business why I'm in jail, and I dare anybody to write anything about me."

"No problem," Belinda stammered.

Willa, a 17-year-old senior, who was everybody's friend and the most popular girl in her class, was probably the most mature girl in the group. Some girls had whispered that she even dated teachers.

She said, "I'm here because I can't afford not to be."

"Very mature," Bonnie mouthed when I made the mistake of glancing in her direction.

A 15-year-old 10th grader, Jeannie, who seemed to have a "nervous condition" of some kind and also was very insecure, worried about what people thought of her or what they might be saying about her. She rambled on for several minutes but never made it clear why she had marched.

"How confusing," Bonnie said.

Tricher, a very energetic, self-confident 17-year-old senior, who was a majorette and vice president of the student government at Monroe, said, "My mother volunteers with the movement and I've been involved from the beginning. This is the second time I've been to jail because I believe in the cause and will do whatever is needed to support it. If we don't fight, we won't win."

Bonnie, the now-confirmed peanut gallery, said, "Impressive."

Some of the girls said that 16-year-old 11th grade cousins, Tammy and Shelma, who were the next interviewees, were "boy crazy" and that they were silly-acting. They were giggling when they said, almost simultaneously, "We marched because our boyfriends didn't believe we would. We showed them!"

I immediately looked at the peanut gallery for a reaction: "Empty heads," she said

Cubicle 5 housed six girls. I only knew them as a group and didn't bother them. They were from the west side of town and I felt a little uneasy around them. They called Belinda to their cubicle instead of coming out to the table like everybody else was doing. Belinda, with pen and paper in hand, walked to the opening of their cubicle. I didn't go because they didn't call my name. They began talking loudly before she could ask a question. The best way to describe their comments is to say not only could I not write the things they said, I didn't even know how to spell some of them! And if White people had heard them, I think they would have handed them their freedom on a silver platter.

Belinda soon backed away from their cubicle and returned to the table. She clearly looked rattled by that encounter, which caused my mind to start racing.

Their words were the most vile I'd ever heard. Make no mistake—a lot of the girls had been cursing during our time in jail. I even tried to string together a combo, but Bonnie told me to stick with what I knew because the two words I put together didn't match. She had said, "Cursing is an art, SavannahBelle. You gotta do it in a way that commands authority. Certain combinations are made to do just that. You just can't make up a phrase and think you'll get respect. *And*, you have to have the right voice for cursing."

I thought I had heard my dad use the combination I tried. Whatever it was that he said, it got our attention at home. That's for sure! But I decided I'd leave cursing alone since I was already in deep trouble on the home front and didn't need to add anything else to my list of offenses.

All of these things made me think—on the one hand, our freedom had been taken away when we were arrested, but on the other hand, we were free to do and say anything we wanted because there was no adult supervision. Of course, there were the jail guards and police officers, but within the confines of the cell, it was just us teenagers. We were free to lounge around doing nothing all day, stay up all night if that was our desire, sleep as late as we wanted, never take a shower, never get dressed, sleep in our clothes, fuss and fight, never have to do chores, and even use curse words. This kind of behavior was outside the boundaries of everything I had been taught. In fact, my parents, grandparents, teachers, or other adults had always told me what I could or could not do. Even though the jail experience was new and, at times, exciting, I realized, even at 13, that I wouldn't want to live an unproductive and unstructured life.

Back to Belinda and our task: she leaned over and whispered, "Those girls can make their own place in history, without our help."

"Amen," I muttered back to her.

Surprisingly, several more girls were in line waiting to be interviewed as Belinda tried to compose herself. She seemed a little nervous.

Next up was a very quiet girl with whom I had had no interaction. She was Kathy, 16 years old in the 11th grade. She began responding in a very soft voice to Belinda's question about why she had marched.

"I don't want to go to school with White students. I don't want to live in a White neighborhood or ride in the front of the bus. And, Lord knows, I don't want to go to their White churches."

"Okay. So what do you want?" I questioned.

Her voice rising with emotion, she continued, "The only thing I want, and I dream of that day all the time, is something for my grandma. She lives down in the country on what used to be a farm. There's no one to do any farming since my granddaddy and uncle died, so it's just bare land. I want to dress my grandma up and bring her to town on Washington Street to Kress five-and-ten store. I want us to sit at that lunch counter and order cheeseburgers with lots of onions on them, French fries, and tall glasses of Pepsi Cola. My grandma has never been out to eat. If that's the only thing that comes out of my staying in jail, I'll be happy. It'll be my dream come true."

Bonnie, who was no longer sitting beside me but instead was across the table from me, brushed her finger under her eyes as if wiping away tears, said, "I like her."

Seventeen-year-old Adel, a senior, was next. "You know, I never intended to march. I found myself going to the mass meeting last Saturday night because there was nothing else to do. When they closed the teen center this year, we didn't have any place to go or anything fun to do on Friday and Saturday nights. I honestly got caught up in the preaching and singing, especially the singing, and before I knew what was happening, I was in the line marching to city hall. I'm glad I did it because I really went with my feelings."

The mentioning of the closing of the teen center brought angry comments from many of the girls about how cruel the city was for shutting down the only recreation spot for Negro teenagers. To prevent the integration of the city's two recreation centers, one for Whites and one for Negroes, the city closed both of them. Everybody knew that White kids had access to private clubs that even suspended their membership requirements to let the kids use the facilities. But Negro teens had no alternatives. There would not even be an end-of-summer water show at the teen center and pool, something everybody enjoyed.

All of this was happening as I was experiencing my first year as a teenager. There would be no sock hops at the teen center. I had no idea how I could properly mature without these coveted activities. The sock hops at school just weren't the same, especially because the teachers stood around watching our every move.

Malissa, another 15-year-old 10th grader, said she had marched because she wanted to help end segregation. "I hadn't counted on being put in jail, though. I thought, even after we were arrested, I would be released because I'm a minor, just as many others here are. This is a scary experience and the only reason I haven't bailed out is because everybody is sticking together."

"Hang tough, girl" and "Amen to sticking together" were comments from some of the girls.

A 17-year-old junior named Elizabeth said, "I just can't resist being a part of big history-making events. Y'all may already know that I was the first Negro to ride the escalator in the Sears and Roebuck store when it opened 5 years ago. It's just my nature!"

There was laughter throughout the jail. I couldn't resist chuckling either after those ridiculous remarks.

Another 17-year-old senior, Maria, was next. She was a little arrogant and had been heard saying that she had no patience for the immaturity of many of the girls. "Grow up" was her response to a lot of the silliness most of us found funny and entertaining.

She said, "I don't mind the sacrifice now because I'm preparing for my future, which doesn't include sitting at the back of buses or being a second-class citizen or having the sales woman in Belk's insist that I buy the red fox shade of stockings when I want to buy a lighter shade. She told me that red fox was ordered for colored girls and the other shades were for White ladies. I look forward to the day I can throw them back in her face and get the color that matches my complexion. I don't ever intend to be at the beck-and-call of White people. I plan to be a doctor and be my own boss," she said with pride.

"On what planet, honey?" someone yelled from Cubicle 5.

Another 15-year-old sophomore, Connie, said, "I have to tell the truth and I hope y'all won't laugh at me. I didn't know too much about the purpose of the movement until I got to jail. I had thought it would help Negro people move to better houses. I was going to ask them at the church what my mama needed to do to apply, but everybody was so excited 'til I didn't get a chance. Then I ended up marching out the church with everybody else and being locked up. I really had thought that the movement would help my family move out of the two-room house we live in. If you never lived in a two-room house, no, a two-room shack, you wouldn't understand."

"A lot of 'em understand, girl, even if they don't admit it," someone yelled, again from Cubicle 5.

She continued, "When I go to those White folks' house to help my mama clean and wash, I can't believe all the rooms and beautiful furniture they have. I just stand and stare 'cause it looks so beautiful. Sometimes my mama catches me staring and tells me to get those crazy thoughts out of my head about living like White folks. But I just want something even just one fifth as nice as what they have. And when I leave their house and go back to our little shack, I hate it more and more. Sometimes I just cry. So, y'all see, that's why I'm so sad knowing that the movement won't be able to help my family."

"Wait, I wouldn't say the movement can't help your family," Tricher jumped in. "Even though it may not be as direct or as soon as you or any of us want, in the long run, the movement will help us get better houses because we will have better jobs and make more money. So you shouldn't be sad or ashamed. Your coming here is an investment in your life, in your family's life, and in the entire Negro race."

"So true, so true," other girls agreed.

Then Dean, one of my cubicle mates, who was 16 and a junior, said that her mother was the one who really wanted to march but knew that she would lose her job if she did.

"So I marched for my mama. She's a maid for this rich White family who owns the bank. Mama said Mr. Ogletree hinted many times that she should not get involved with those outside agitators who were trying to make Negroes think they were not being treated right in Albany.

Mama said he asked her, 'Now Rubee, what is it I haven't done for you that you think those agitators can do? Haven't I done right by you and your young-uns? We put clothes on your backs, food on your table, and I even hired two of your gals to shell peas out at the farm last summer and let your boy clean the bank a few times. What else do Negroes want? I say you better be thankful for all you got.'"

"Mama says she just says, 'Yes sir.'"

"See that's the kind of bull I hate," Videl shouted. "Who do they think they are — God? How can this man tell your mama to be thankful when she doesn't have anything, can't get anything, and has to wait on him hand and foot for a lousy buck? This is what makes me so mad!"

"You see," Trudy chimed in, "This is the kind of expression and dialogue I think should be going on. This is good. I don't think that we should hold back our feelings."

"Just listen to that baloney," Patty yelled out in a cutting tone from Cubicle 5.

The interview with Dean concluded our interviews. Belinda thanked everybody and reiterated, "Everybody knows this was voluntary. It was not to embarrass anybody or put anybody down. It's a way for us to have a record for the future."

I thanked Belinda for asking me to help her. We decided to review our notes individually and start putting the article together when we returned home. I was so excited about working with her.

After dinner, the boys yelled for more snacks. We went through the same routine of them lowering the shirt for us to pile snacks into it and sending it back up to them. It was a pretty neat way to communicate with them and everybody was glad to share what we had.

We later started singing freedom songs and could hear the boys join in. We were feeding off our experience from the day before when Dr. King, our families, and other visitors had come to see us. We got louder and louder and started banging on the walls and bars to make sure the boys could hear us and know how excited we were. We could hear them stomping and banging on things, too.

None of us gave any thought to how the guards might react to our spur-of-moment outburst. After about 15 minutes of our singing, the boys abruptly became quiet. Not knowing what was happening, we started shouting to them, encouraging them to continue the celebration. They didn't respond. Then suddenly we heard a scream. At first, we thought it was the boys responding to us, so we yelled encouragement. Then we heard a second scream and we knew that it was a scream of pain, not joy.

We gathered closer to the windows and heard what sounded like several boys screaming in pain. We were frightened and started yelling and asking them what was happening, what was wrong. Then we heard dogs barking and more screaming.

Within minutes, we heard the slamming of doors leading to our cell. We looked in anticipation at the door as it finally opened. In walked four guards with two huge dogs. The officers glared at us with fire in their eyes. They ordered us to get back to our cubicles. As we scrambled to hurriedly return to our bunks, the guards began moving toward us with the dogs right on the heels of some of the girls.

With all the commotion, one of the younger girls, Kate, whose cubicle was near the back, was a little slow in reaching her bunk so one of the guards hit her on the shoulder with his billy club. She let out a wail that told us how painful the blow was.

"Shut up if you know what's good for you!" he said to her and then told one of the officers holding a dog to take it into the girl's cubicle. The dog began barking and leaping forward as the girls in that cubicle moved away from the edge of their bunks.

The two guards, who were not restraining the dogs very well, then paced from one end of the cell to the other. They let the dogs move within each cubicle as they barked and leaped close to the bunks, almost touching the girls who were on the lower bunks.

"Who do you think you are, making a disturbance in my jail? You not in Albany; you in Camilla in my jail! I need to show you what we do with trash like you. I will string you up one by one if we have to come back in here."

Another continued in a deeper pitched voice, "You think because we let that nigger preacher come out there yesterday that you can turn this place out. There won't be any more visitors. We were nice to you, and you show us just what jungle beasts you really are. You belong in cages!"

The first one, who sounded like he could have been the chief, added, "We just made examples of some of those boys so they all understand this ain't a game and we mean business. We won't hesitate to do the same with every one of you."

They put the fear of God in us and when they finally left, many of the girls were crying. I was more frightened than I had ever been. In a matter of minutes, we went from being jubilant to boot-shaking scared.

A couple of the girls were consoling Kate and rubbing her shoulder where the officer hit her; her shoulder had already developed a large knot and she cried on and on and on.

"I can't stand to think about how badly the boys may have been hurt," Tricher said.

No one did much talking that night. Trudy's prayers were just above a whisper.

I stayed on my bunk the rest of the night and began writing about what had happened. Just as I would always remember Dr. King's visit the day before, I would remember tonight's episode for the rest of my life.

CHAPTER EIGHT

Early on Thursday morning, probably about 6 o'clock, Benny came into the corridor behind our cell with his mop and bucket. One of the older girls called him over and asked if he knew anything about what happened to the boys and whether any of them were hurt.

"They been moved," he said nonchalantly.

"Moved? Moved where?" she asked.

"I don't know nothing else."

"Benny, please tell us," several girls begged.

"I don't know nothing to tell you."

"Can you find out and let us know?"

"Okay, okay. Y'all better be careful, though. They saw y'all sending food upstairs through the window, and they took all they hadn't already ate when they went in there. Anyway, forget about that. I figured y'all needed some cheering up this morning, so I brought my radio to let you listen to it."

" What? A radio?"

He plugged it in and turned it up real loud. We hadn't heard any music, except from our own singing, since we'd been locked up. The songs being played were what we called hillbilly numbers. They made me feel sadder and more depressed than I already was feeling.

Someone from Cubicle 5 shouted choice words to Benny, telling him to turn off the radio because they were trying to sleep!

Benny ignored them as he began mopping the long corridor. He always took a long time whenever he came into the corridor because, I believe, he had an ulterior motive; he enjoyed looking at us girls in various forms of undress. The only cubicle he could not see into was the first one because it had a solid wall to accommodate the toilet. The rest of us tried to shield each other whenever he suddenly appeared, especially early in the mornings.

After several songs, the station played an old number that made all of us come to life. It was "This Magic Moment" by the Drifters:

> "This magic moment, so different and so new,
> Unlike any other, until I met you.
> And then it happened, it took me by surprise,
> Oh, I think that you felt it, too,
> By the look in your eyes.

Then all of us joined in —

Sweeter than wine,
Softer than the summer night. . . .

And with even more harmony —

Everything I <u>want</u> I have,
Whenever I hold you tight . . .

Someone cried out, "Oh, help me, I can't stand it!"

Seeing how much everybody was enjoying the Drifters, Benny turned the sound down so that we couldn't hear anything.

"Don't turn it off, please, Benny, please," we begged.

"Naw, y'all told me to turn it off."

"You turkey! You don't have to let us listen. That's okay. Be nasty!" someone yelled.

No one else said anything; we stopped begging.

Realizing that we weren't going to play his game with him, he turned the volume up again, just as the song was ending. But immediately following the Drifters came Maxine Brown with "All in My Mind." The DJ at the station must have known that there were some Negro girls out there who were hungry to hear some good music.

I don't know, baby, maybe it's all in my mind.
We've been going steady so long,
I never dreamed you'd ever do me wrong.
I knew I was yours, and I thought you were mine,

And, ah, every little thing was so fine.
Oh, Oh, darling, I hate to see
Someone else with you, other than me. . .

It felt so good to be able to listen to some of our favorite
songs, but the station went right back to playing hillbilly
music. After another two or three of those numbers, though,
we were surprised again. "C. C. Rider" by Chuck Willis
came on. It was an older song but still popular.

We didn't even have to ask Benny to turn the volume up this
time. This song had a good beat and most of us jumped
off our bunks and started dancing. We were doing the slop,
a slow-pace twist, and swinging with each other. We were
having a ball, singing and dancing to the beat, which
sounded like a piccolo playing:

Just see, C. C. Rider
Girl, see what you have done.
Yes, yes see, C. C. Rider
See what you have done.
Girl, you made me love you
Now your man has come.

Well I'm going away, baby
And I won't be back till the fall.
Yes darling, I'm going away, baby
Won't be back until fall.
If I find me a good girl,
I won't be back at all.

Well see, C. C. Rider
Girl, the moon is shining bright.
Lord, Lord, Lord, see C. C. Rider,
The moon is shining bright.
If I could just walk with you
Everything would be alright.
C. C. Rider, C. C. Rider. . .

Benny started trying to dance after seeing that we were having so much fun. This reminded me of being at Grand Vann's house and hearing the piccolo at Mr. Boot's café and the ladies laughing and having a great time.

This was a good way to get the day started after what happened the previous night. In fact, many of the girls were glad when the guards brought breakfast because they had worked up an appetite.

Bonnie said, laughing, "I didn't work hard enough to want to eat what they're serving."

Around mid-morning, 17-year-old Maria complained that she didn't feel well. She was having horrible stomach cramps and had a throbbing headache. She didn't eat anything for breakfast and had hardly touched her dinner last night. Someone offered her some of their snacks but she said she just couldn't eat.

Among the supplies Dr. King and his group brought was a large bottle of aspirin. She had taken a couple last night and two more this morning. She finally fell asleep early in the afternoon.

Another younger girl, Kitty, also complained that she felt
sick. She had a headache. She took a couple of aspirin and
slept for a few hours.

At around 9:00 that evening, Maria began throwing up and
was as hot as an oven, one of her cubicle mates informed us.
She had started moaning and groaning. Someone had a coke
and told her to sip some of it. She threw that up.

About a half hour later, some of the girls decided that she
needed medical attention because she was not getting better.
We were sensitive to the consequences of yelling and
noisemaking, but we made a conscious decision that we
needed to do whatever would get the attention of the guards
since it was unlikely anyone would be coming to check on
us before morning. Having no idea how close or far away
the guards were, some of the girls began yelling for help,
trying to get the guards' attention. Most of us joined in,
getting louder and louder. We beat on the bars, screamed,
clapped our hands, and did everything we could think of,
hoping that someone would hear us. We didn't even know
whether there were guards on the premises. We began to
panic and just screamed and screamed. This went on for 30
or 40 minutes.

Finally, we heard the chains and doors opening. We
anxiously awaited the opening of the steel door to our cell.
Everyone's eyes were on that door. When it finally opened,
the guards came in with their billy clubs in hand and started
yelling and cursing at us.

"Sir, sir," interrupted Trudy in a nervous voice, "A couple of
the girls are real sick and need to see a doctor. We didn't
know what else to do."

The three guards turned around and walked out of the cell and closed the steel door. Everyone remained quiet but puzzled. We didn't know what that meant.

About 15 or 20 minutes passed before we heard them unlocking the steel door again. They stood at the entrance and one of them asked, "Which ones of y'all so sick?"

To the surprise of many of us, not only did Maria and Kitty, the two who were sick, rise and identify themselves, but two more girls, both from Cubicle 5, claimed that they were ill, too.

"What are they doing?" I asked Bonnie under my breath.

The guard told the four of them to come with him. Maria, who was the sickest, needed help walking so the two impostors assisted her.

As soon as the door slammed shut, the four remaining girls in Cubicle 5 told us that the reason the two girls claimed to be sick was because they wanted to go home and this was their way out. The remaining girls, including Patty, said they had been reluctant to fake sickness but wished they had since it had gone so smoothly. Patty said that they all were tired of the nasty food and were getting restless.

I became depressed after I heard those comments. We had made a commitment to stick together. The girls who were truly ill could not control that, and I was glad they would be able to go home, but I was disappointed that the other two faked their illness. I sat at the table, feeling sad and betrayed.

Suddenly, we heard the chains being taken off the doors again. We hadn't been making any noise, so we couldn't imagine why the guards were coming back. About 30 minutes had passed since the girls left. When the steel door opened, all four girls came back into the cell and they all were sobbing. Only one was assisting Maria. We rushed to them as soon as the door closed.

"What's wrong, what happened?" We all asked at once.

"We thought y'all might have been half way home by now."

Maria said that they were taken to a room and left alone for about 15 minutes.

"Finally," she said between sobs, "A man dressed in some khaki pants and a blue shirt and carrying a black brief case, came in the room with the guards. He said he was a doctor. Then he pulled out a needle. Oh, Lord, Oh, Jesus," she started sobbing louder.

Kitty added, "He stuck that long needle into a bottle that had a pinkish liquid."

"It looked like dishwashing soap," one of the impostors screamed.

"He then took each one of us by the arm and injected that liquid, with force, into our arms," Maria continued in a frightened voice.

The other imposter said, "That man did not change needles and did not wipe our arms like they do at school when we get shots."

"He didn't sterilize the needle or clean our arms. He went from one of us to the next without changing needles. I have never heard of anything like this in my life. That was the biggest needle I have ever seen. I believe they use that size needle on horses," Kitty cried.

"Jesus, Jesus, help us, Lord," Trudy pleaded.

The most horrifying part of the whole ordeal, to me, was that he used the same needle on all of them.

All of the girls said that this so-called doctor actually had a smile on his face as they cried out in pain. After he gave the last shot, the guards told them that if that didn't shut them up, they had something else for them.

Their arms were bleeding. The "doctor" had not put a bandage on the area nor had he given them anything to stop the bleeding.

None of us could believe what we were hearing. Someone whose credentials were justifiably questionable had injected the girls with an unknown liquid from the same contaminated needle. This was the most incredible thing we had experienced! All four girls were crying and their arms were still bleeding.

Willa, one of the older girls, told us to wet some tissue and apply it with pressure to their arms. This was repeated as the tissue became bloody, and eventually the bleeding stopped. However, the crying and pain did not.

When we were back in our cubicle, Bonnie and Jackie began snickering at the two impostors, saying they got what they deserved.

"How can you say that? What happened to them was cruel," I whispered.

"Everybody knows you don't go blindly into a dark alley. Whatever gave them the idea they were going to let them go home?" Bonnie continued whispering.

"They may have gotten some kind of disease from that needle. If their arms are swollen tomorrow, don't touch them," Jackie warned.

"What?" I questioned, alarmed.

"Infection! Infection! It could be contagious!" Jackie said a little louder than our whispers.

Before I could question her further, Trudy asked for everyone's attention, which was pretty easy to get at that moment. She said she thought prayer was needed and asked everyone to bow their heads because one of the older girls, Elaine, was going to pray.

"Dear God, Dear Jesus," Elaine began. "Here we are again to ask you to help us hold on and stay together. We know you will always protect us. We know you chose us to bear this burden at this time because we are young and our backs are strong. We won't give up. Lord, we know that this small sacrifice we are making will help our race. It will help our mamas from slaving all day in White folks' kitchens for $30 a week, and it will give them the courage to refuse to call little White girls 'Miss' and boys 'Mr.,' while these children call them by their first names. We know, Dear God, that it will help our daddies refuse to answer to 'boy' and 'uncle' and to look White men in the eye. We want respect for our parents, Oh God. We don't want them to have to bow their heads and keep their eyes downcast.

"Lord, have mercy, and help us keep our sight on the cause of freedom. We know there is a brighter day ahead. We, we, we just believe it! And please, please, Dear God, heal the girls who are sick tonight. We pray that whatever they were injected with tonight will not poison their blood stream. And please forgive the two who pretended they were sick. They didn't mean any harm. Lord, we ask you to continue to guide and bless us. Amen."

We were all saying amen again and again. There were few dry eyes among us.

I continued to be amazed by the powerful prayers some of the girls prayed. This was so different from what I had ever heard from a child. The Lord's Prayer, bedtime prayers, grace, Christmas program prayers, and Easter prayers were about the extent of children's prayers I'd ever heard, and I went to church all the time. I just had never heard children or young people pray like Trudy and the other girls prayed, with such emotion and conviction.

Many of the girls put their arms around Elaine because I think she was going to shout. She definitely had touched the pulse of the group.

When it was time for us to lie down for the night, Maria said she still wasn't feeling any better, but at least she wasn't moaning as loudly. Nobody slept much and several of the girls took turns checking on both girls, putting wet tissue on their arms and foreheads and giving them drinks of water. Hearts had softened for the two impostors and their arms were tended to as well. We came together as a team that night.

All of the tension was taking a toll on me, however. I found myself humming "Mary Had A Little Lamb" and "Yankee Doodle Dandy," one after the other. That was a sure sign I was nervous or afraid; in this case, both. As long as I could remember, I hummed those songs when I was in a terrible situation. My humming got louder and faster. I was sitting on the top bunk; Bonnie was lying across in a semi ball or fetal position.

> *Mary had a little lamb, little lamb, little lamb. Mary had a little lamb with fleece as white as snow.*

On and on I hummed and rocked back and forth.

"What *is* wrong with you, SavannahBelle? Are you flipping out?" Bonnie asked, leaning on her elbow in a slight sitting position.

I didn't respond; I just kept humming and rocking.

"SavannahBelle," she said as she shook me, "You're scaring me with that weird noise and those psychotic moves. Stop it!"

CHAPTER NINE

On Friday morning, Kitty felt better but Maria was not doing well at all. The stomachache had become sharp cramps by now, and she was still bothered by the throbbing headache. She tried to look cheerful and said her headache was a little less annoying, but she was burning up with fever. All four of the girls who were injected with the unknown solution had swollen and sore arms. That concerned everybody, especially the girls in Cubicle 5, as to whether the unsterilized needle would cause infection, or had already caused it, and whether the solution would have harmful effects on them. These were nagging questions and thoughts, and none of us could answer them.

Some of the older girls, Trudy, Tricher, Belinda, and Elaine, decided that regardless of whatever harm might come to them, they had to try again to get some medical attention for Maria. They thought that it would be better in her case to go home.

At breakfast call, Belinda, who was chosen to be our spokesperson, asked the guards in rapid succession if it would be possible to get word to Maria's parents because she was desperately ill, and she seemed to need to be hospitalized, and we were afraid, because her temperature was so high, that she might go into convulsions and die. Belinda placed a lot of emphasis on the word "die." She seemed out of breath when she finished.

We were shocked when one of the guards wrote down Maria's name and her home telephone number. This happened around 7:30 in the morning. At 11:00 o'clock, someone was there to pick her up. We were so relieved and wished her a speedy recovery. Everybody hugged her and helped her gather the few things she had there.

Some of the girls told her to call their parents to let them know they were doing fine. They also warned her not to tell her parents or anyone else what had happened to us because they feared that the parents might panic and think we couldn't handle being in jail.

"Girl, you get well. We'll call to check on you when we get out," Trudy told her.

Everyone was so relieved that she was able to go home to get proper medical attention.

Later that morning, when Benny appeared in the corridor, we bombarded him with questions about what was happening with the boys. Initially, he said he hadn't found out anything more about them. Martha, whose boyfriend was in the group, was desperate to hear some news. She played on Benny's ego, falsely portraying him as a big man with a lot of power and someone to whom we all looked up.

She whispered to him in a sexy tone, "I understand if you can't tell the secrets of the jail. After all, a big man in your position has to be careful."

Then Betty, one of her friends, picking up on the game being run on Benny, used reverse psychology by saying sarcastically, "I don't believe he knows anything. I bet they don't let him in on jail secrets. I don't think he's a real trustee."

That did it! Benny didn't want to give the impression that he wasn't in the know, being the only trustee the jail had. We don't know whether he was telling the truth or just making up things to impress us, but he said, "They in the county jail. Two or three of 'em got hurt kinda bad and had to go to the clinic and get stitches. They all right now and back in the cell."

"What?" several girls asked.

"Shh," others told them. "We don't want Benny to get in trouble telling us this stuff."

The girls thought they were pulling a fast one on Benny. I learned at that moment that game playing can be a dangerous thing for amateurs. Although Martha, who used the sexy tone, normally would have been the target, Betty was the one standing against the bars. In a flash, Benny reached his hands just inside the bars and quickly squeezed both of her breasts.

"Get your hands off of me you dirty scum ball," she yelled, backing away and hitting at his hands as he laughed and stomped his feet in triumph. He went down to the floor he was so tickled.

Benny took advantage of a situation when the girls had let their guards down and were vulnerable because of their concern about the boys. Benny was a better student of psychology than the girls realized. I guess the lesson for us was to never underestimate your opponent, especially when you are already at a disadvantage. This jail experience was teaching me more psychology than I could possibly ever learn in the classroom.

Most of us had been in jail 6 days, some a few days longer. With Maria's departure, many of the girls started talking about going home, too, something we hadn't allowed ourselves to do up to this point.

I began thinking of how I was going to explain my defiance. Although my mother didn't sound concerned about what I had done when she visited on Tuesday, only expressing an interest in my well-being, I just didn't know what kind of punishment I would face once I got back home. That was what I had avoided dwelling on during the past 6 days.

Suddenly, someone yelled for everybody to come to Cubicle 5.

"Not us," Bonnie and Jackie said, shaking their heads.

"You won't believe what they've done," the girl continued.

"I'll believe anything those roughriders might do," Jackie giggled.

Everybody was shocked when they saw the two walls in the cubicle. They had written on and drawn graffiti about everything and everybody all over the walls, even between the upper and lower beds.

"I wonder if we'll get in trouble when they see this," Dean said.

"Who cares? Why don't we all leave something for them to read, especially since we won't have this opportunity ever again in life," somebody else said.

Everybody seemed to like the idea.

There were a few markers; it surprised me that we had such tools available, so we began preparing to leave our "legacy."

Back in our cubicle, we decided to write our names, coupled with our boyfriends' names, if we had one, and draw a heart around each pair. Or, as in my case, write the name of the boy you dreamed of and wished you had. But because Steven's girlfriend, Nona, was one of the girls in jail with us, I didn't dare write his name in a heart with mine. So instead, I put the name of a boy named Thomas who lived down the street from Grand Vann in Cuthbert.

Then we came up with a few prophetic lines:

> *You can beat us till we're blue and black--*
> *We'll just keep on marching, we'll be back!"*

> *"Cement walls and jail bars to hold us in--*
> *You may stop us now, but someday we shall win.*

> —67 Strong, July 1962

Bonnie scribbled something on a piece of paper and shoved it in my hand. I laughed aloud when I read it:

> *Freedom now or freedom later –*
> *This is the last you'll see of this alligator.*

Everybody was yelling out their lines and waiting for the markers to write them across the walls. Then we went from cubicle to cubicle, wall to wall, reading what everybody had written. We were reviving our souls.

Jessa said with enthusiasm, "This makes me feel like we're getting justice!"

Belinda said, "Unfortunately, this is probably the only justice we will ever get. Negroes never get fair trials, if we even make it to court, especially in the South, because the laws are written to favor White people. And they love the Jim Crow laws because they are designed to keep us as second class citizens. It's almost as bad as being in slavery when we were the property of White folk."

Tricher added, "My mother said at a meeting in the movement office a couple of weeks ago, they were discussing how the Constitution classifies Negroes as three-fifths human. That's how they justified keeping us as slaves and selling us as property. Can you believe the law let them do all these things?"

Belinda ended by saying, "So, Jessa, we are at the bottom of the barrel when it comes to justice. We have so far to look up for justice that our necks hurt."

The comments from both Belinda and Tricher made us think about how far we had to go in this fight for freedom.

Later in the day, about a dozen girls' names were called. Their bond had been posted and their parents were there to pick them up.

This came as a total surprise to us. Nobody expected to stay in jail the rest of the summer, but we hadn't expected the departures to start at this time or that we wouldn't be released together; we had come in together, so we assumed, I guessed, that we would leave the same way.

"Does this mean that one of us could possibly be left in here alone?" Willa asked.

Trudy said, "We need a strategy. Everyone needs to write her name and telephone number on this piece of paper. If you don't have a telephone, write down a neighbor's number, a relative's number, or your address on the paper. Those of you who are going home first must contact our parents right away to come and get us. Make that the first thing you do when you get out of here. We can't leave one or two girls in here alone. It would be dangerous for a girl to be left here alone."

As I listened to Trudy, I became terrified. None of this had ever occurred to me. I never thought of being in that kind of danger or being left alone in jail. The very thought of this almost frightened me to death.

We agreed that this was the best approach to take.

Tricher also instructed the girls who were leaving to call her mother immediately. "Tell her we're concerned that, because girls are now going home in big groups, someone may be left here alone and that would be dangerous! We need the movement to know our concern and make sure everybody gets out of here. She'll get the ball rolling."

By late afternoon, a total of 23 girls had left. Bonnie was one of the last names they called on Friday, and I cried as she was leaving. She said she would call my mother and let her know that I was ready to come home, too.

There was a somber mood in the jail that evening. We sensed that the end was near, that we had served the intended purpose. Almost everyone now had a bed to herself. I lay on my bunk and thought about going home.

On the one hand, I was now looking forward to getting out of jail; on the other hand, I wasn't sure what kind of punishment to expect. I knew it would be harsh and I knew I would never forget it. I had it coming to me; it was self-inflicted. Even so, I'd rather face that punishment than be left in jail alone.

Someone starting singing and that caught my attention. It was so soft and sweet.

> *This little light of mine, I'm gonna let it shine.*
> *Oh, this little light of mine, I'm gonna let it shine.*
> *This little light of mine, I'm gonna let it shine, let it*
> *shine, let it shine, let it shine.*
>
> *Everywhere I go, Lord, I'm gonna let it shine.*
> *Oh, everywhere I go, I'm gonna let it shine.*
> *Everywhere I go, I'm gonna let it shine, let it shine,*
> *let it shine, let it shine.*
>
> *All in the jailhouse, I'm gonna let it shine.*
> *Oh, all in the jailhouse, I'm gonna let it shine.*
> *All in the jail house, I'm gonna let it shine, let it*
> *shine, let it shine, let it shine.*
>
> *On the streets of Albany, I'm gonna let it shine.*
> *Oh, on the streets of Albany, I'm gonna let it shine.*

On the streets of Albany, I'm gonna let it shine, let it shine, let it shine, let it shine.

I'm gonna let my little light shine.

The singing settled my nerves and really lifted my spirit. I felt ready to face whatever my fate might be.

CHAPTER TEN

Later that night, I had what I considered a recurring nightmare. I was never sure whether these encounters were real or a dream. I labeled them a nightmare because I felt a sense of comfort believing it was only a figment of my subconscious. Mama also had told me they were just bad dreams and nothing to be frightened about. However, I had had these nightmares for the past 5 years.

At first, they happened about once a year, but now they were occurring every 3 or 4 months. They were always the same, though. I would hear footsteps on the sidewalk leading to the front porch of our house. I would hear the key turn the lock and the front door open, then close, and footsteps would come down the hallway to my bedroom. I could hear deliberate footsteps, like they were weighed down. The intruder would enter my bedroom and walk to my bed. Although there was another bed in the room — Larene's bed — the intruder always came to my bed. I could feel the heat from its body as it stood there. My face would always be turned toward the wall, with my back to the door, and I could never turn over to see it. I could only see its shadow on the wall as it spread what appeared to be wings high above my bed.

I always tried to turn over or even roll off the bed to hide under it, but I could never move. It had a foul, sickening odor. I would be in total distress and paralyzed with fear. Then it would start making sounds. I would scream for help but I couldn't hear my voice; no sound ever actually came from my mouth. It seemed as if I were in a silent movie, suffocating.

I had always been afraid of ghost stories and talk about dead people. That was so ironic because our house was surrounded by three cemeteries, and I witnessed funeral processions and burials usually a couple of times a week. I often wondered if this intruder was a dead person trying to go back home and needed directions.

I was 8 years old when my great, great Aunt Lodie died. She was Grand Vann's aunt. It was in July 1957 and I was visiting Grand Vann for a few weeks before school started. Grand Vann and I rushed to Aunt Lodie's house because someone came and told Grand Vann that it wouldn't be long and she should hurry. When we arrived, Aunt Lodie had already died and her next door neighbor had put a pillow case under her chin and tightly tied it on top of her head. I didn't go in the room, but I heard that this had to do with some ritual to keep her mouth from gaping open. Grand Vann expressed anger because she said no one had a right to interfere with Aunt Lodie's body. She said Aunt Lodie may not have been dead at the time that "noose" choked her.

Aunt Lodie was the first dead person I had actually seen close up in a casket. My mother's father, Daddy Gus, died the year before but I never saw him in his casket. Grand Vann and I went to the funeral home to view Aunt Lodie's body the day before her funeral. The viewing room was small with heavy dark draperies. It was dimly lit and hot. The casket was placed on a tall stand. It had a full glass top that seemingly sealed her inside, and her body was placed very low in it. I had to get on my tip-toes to look down in the casket. I gasped when I saw her and lost my balance, which caused me to fall against the casket. She looked so small, wrinkled, and powdery, and her head seemed to be pulled back. She actually looked like a mummy, and I was scared beyond words. All I could think of was Grand Vann's comments about that pillow case being tied around her head choking her. Suddenly, I couldn't breathe. I struggled to swallow. I was choking! I panicked. There was nothing for me to do but turn and run the four blocks back to Grand Vann's house to get some water. I was hyperventilating by the time I reached the house.

I quickly gulped down two glasses of water and was still gasping for air when Grand Vann rushed in the house.

"What in the world is wrong with you, SavannahBelle? You ran out of that funeral parlor like you were on fire."

I could tell she was upset with me. "I'm sorry, Grand Vann. I couldn't breathe. I don't like to look at dead people," I cried.

Since that episode, I have avoided looking at dead people; but because for many years we lived in a house surrounded by cemeteries, I am forever reminded that they exist and that they are an intriguing mystery. They are a source of fear and imagination for me.

But on this night in jail, the encounter with the intruder was different with unimaginable results. The intruder seemed confused as it entered the big steel door of the jail. I heard the door open and close and knew immediately what it was. But its footsteps sounded confused. It went to two cubicles, quickly exiting, before making its way to mine and to my bed. Since I was on the top bunk, it had to hoist itself off the floor over my bed.

The smell was more sickening than ever. I couldn't see its full shadow on the wall because of its elevated position. Its frame seemingly faded onto the ceiling. It seemed angry and made much louder noises than usual. As always, I was facing the wall, with my back to the entrance. Suddenly, although frightened beyond words, I didn't feel paralyzed. I felt free and with a small sense of power. I couldn't believe that I was actually beginning to slowly turn my body over. I didn't want to make a sudden move and have this thing harm me. I eased over on my back and after a few seconds, mustered the courage to turn my face toward this intruder.

Right in front of my eyes was the most grotesque sight I had ever seen. I screamed down in my throat, making a frightening sound that I didn't recognize as my own. The bed seemed to be vibrating, and thick black smoke suddenly was billowing above the bed.

I was looking at a disfigured monster that was, I would guess, at least 6 feet tall, with a slight crookedness about it. It had a long skinny face, and its mouth, which was covered in green foam, came to a sharp point. Large black holes were where the eyes should have been. It had long arms with wide wing spans. But there were no hands. I couldn't see its legs or whether it had feet. It was black, but I couldn't tell whether it was hair or skin that was black.

My mouth was making screaming motions but the initial sound I had been able to make had stopped, and I now was on my knees with my back against the wall; tears were streaming down my face and my arms were flailing in the air as I tried to protect myself.

The light from the corridor, which usually made the cell extremely bright, seemed quite dim on this night, except over my bed, where it was brighter than it had ever been. It was as if the light had been provided for me so that I could get a good look at this monster.

The expression on its face seemed to be apologetic, as if it were begging me not to be afraid. Even those winged arms were lowered as it stared at me. Then, suddenly, the black cloud of smoke descended over it and within seconds engulfed it. It extended its arms toward me, as if pleading for help, or forgiveness, or maybe even understanding.

I continued to try to push back against the wall, although I couldn't physically move any further back. It was impossible for me to put any more distance between us, yet I kept pushing against the cinder blocks. I had gotten extremely cold and my whole body was trembling.

The cloud continued to descend and everything disappeared from my sight. I assumed it landed on the floor beside the lower bunk bed where Jackie slept. I was in too much shock and fear to think rationally.

Then there was a loud blast, like a bomb exploding. I folded my body over and covered my head and ears with my arms. We didn't have sheets or blankets, so there was nothing I could use to shield myself from this horrible scene. I was too terrified to look.

I expected the other girls to jump out of their beds and come running to see what was going on, but no one made a sound. It seemed that everybody was still asleep, including Jackie,

Dee-Dee, and Pat, right there in the cubicle with me. Dean had already moved to another cubicle, so it was just the four of us now.

I stayed in this protective position for what seemed like hours. Usually, Benny came into the corridor before breakfast, perhaps around 6:00 or 6:30 some mornings. This was one time I was looking forward to seeing him.

Jackie awoke before Benny came into the corridor, however. I heard her say, more to herself than anyone else, "What the heck is all this stuff on the floor? Who put this mess by my bed?"

I was not anxious to look or engage in discussion about the trauma I had experienced just hours earlier, so I said nothing. Besides, the way I was still trembling, I knew my voice would be a dead giveaway.

Dee-Dee heard Jackie and was more dramatic in her expressions, "Good Lord, what burned up in here? Somebody had a fire right here in the middle of the floor. This mess stinks!"

I found the courage to say, "What's going on?" But, I didn't move to get a look at the floor.

"What's going on? Look at this floor and smell this foul odor that seems to be getting stronger," Dee-Dee said.

Some of the other girls were stirring about now and came to the opening of our cubicle to see what was happening.

Everybody was saying about the same thing.

"What did y'all do in here last night? It smells like you cooked a darn skunk," Videl said as she backed away from our cubicle holding her nose and gagging.

I eased over to the edge of my bunk and almost collapsed when I looked down on the floor. There was a huge circle of burned debris. It looked as if someone had set something afire and it had burned to a crisp. The floor was cement but it looked like a hole had been burned into it.

"This thing is smoldering," Jackie said in disbelief, backing away from it.

"You four girls have gone too far," Trudy said after peering into the entrance to our cubicle. "Y'all could get all of us in trouble. Where did you even get matches and what was this mess you burned? You could have killed all of us!"

Pat, upset at Trudy's accusation, said, "Hold on a minute, sister! We haven't done anything. You know we don't have any matches. If we had set a fire, wouldn't all of you have smelled smoke? This is as much a mystery to us as it is to everybody else. Don't start any lies about us setting a fire in here."

"Could someone have come in here while we were asleep and done this?"

"All of y'all need to calm down. Benny will be coming down that corridor any minute and he will certainly call in the guards if he sees this mess," Martha said.

Trudy said nervously, "You're right, you're right. First, we need to put something over this. I know, let's drag one of the extra mattresses in here and cover this hole with it."

"Wait, if it's still smoldering, that would only start a worse fire than we've already had," Jackie warned.

"Let's get some water and pour on it first," Pat suggested.

It seemed that team work had kicked in again. However, I was afraid to say anything because I didn't think anyone would believe me, especially with my voice trembling. I was still trying to recuperate from the unbelievable and insane confrontation I had with that monster. I didn't know what any of it meant. I still couldn't believe that I actually turned over and came face-to-face with it! I couldn't believe how horrible it looked and what expressions it had. I was about to freak out thinking about it.

I started quietly praying, "Please, God, don't let us get in trouble. I can't explain this to anybody that would make any sense. I feel responsible but, Lord, it wasn't within my control. I know the guards will punish all of us for damaging the cell. How do we get out of this? Please, please, save us, Jesus. I'll do anything. Thank you, God."

I was still on my bed, afraid to get down, and not saying anything.

"So none of you girls in this cubicle heard, saw, or smelled anything last night?" Videl asked with a bit of disbelief in her voice.

"I was sleeping right here on the bottom bunk closest to this hole and I didn't see, hear, smell, taste, or touch a doggone thing," Jackie said with great indignation.

Dee-Dee and Pat said they had no clue, either. I just shook my head, too scared to speak.

As water was poured over the hole, a puff of smoke rose almost to the ceiling and that awful smell grew stronger. Jackie and Trudy quickly threw the mattress over it, without a minute to spare. Benny opened the door, as if on cue, and came into the corridor.

"My God," he yelled. "What you gals been doing in here this morning? It smell like a polecat done died in here. Good God Ah'mighty!"

"You shut your mouth, Benny. You the one bringing in that awful smell," Patty in Cubicle 5 countered, much to my surprise.

"One thing about it, I don't have to smell this funk all day," he shouted back.

He mopped with ammonia and strong-smelling Lysol as he fussed, but that helped tremendously in getting rid of some of the odor. In fact, when breakfast was brought in around 7:30, we weren't able to detect much of an odor at all from the hole, and the guards didn't say anything. The regular odor we had grown accustomed to was still kicking, however.

I mustered up enough courage to get off the bunk when I realized everyone was going to get in the breakfast line and I would be left in the cubicle alone. I eased off the bunk, put my feet on Jackie's bunk, and stepped as far away from the mattress that covered the hole as I possibly could and flew out of there into the open area of the cell. I had decided that I would not sleep in that cubicle another night, and since there were fewer girls now, I could bunk in another cubicle, as Dean was doing, or sleep on the eating table if necessary.

Right before lunch, Trudy said she was going to check to see if the fire was completely out because she said sometimes smoldering fires will reignite. So she and Jackie pulled the mattress off the hole and all I heard was, "This is unbelievable! I can't believe my eyes!"

"What? What?" someone yelled but said she was too afraid to come and look.

"Come here, quick! You won't believe it."

A few brave girls ran to the entrance of the cubicle and were repeating what Trudy and Jackie had said.

I didn't move. I couldn't imagine! I was waiting for someone to start screaming as they came face-to-face with that monster. I was holding my breath and silently praying.

"It's like there was never a fire or hole here at all. This is too creepy for me!"

"What are you saying?"

"This floor looks like nothing happened here."

Everybody who had seen that floor a few hours earlier was astounded that there now was no evidence of anything. I walked over to the cubicle, knees weak, palms wet, and body trembling, and looked in disbelief, too. If the other girls had not witnessed it, I would have thought I'd dreamed all of it. In a way, I was glad to finally have confirmation of what had been causing havoc in my life these past years.

"How do you explain this?" another asked.

Trudy said, "We don't need to. Let's just forget this ever happened."

I would be happy to do that, but I couldn't take my eyes off that spot on the floor.

CHAPTER ELEVEN

"Savannah Richards, get your stuff and come this way," a loud voice bellowed after the door opened. It was right after lunch. He called some other names but I was oblivious to everything else.

I jumped to attention and scrambled to get my box that already had my few clothes in it. I hugged Jackie, Dee-Dee, Pat, and Dean, as well as Belinda and Trudy, and hurried toward the door.

"Hurry up, we don't have all day," the guard said in a stern voice.

"Call my folks," several girls yelled after us.

I would make that my first order of business.

We were led out of the cell down a long corridor that looked much different on this 28th day of July than it did the week before when we were brought to this jail. Everything looked so much brighter and longer.

When we finally reached an entrance room, I looked around and there was my dad standing there waiting for me. It was not until that moment that I realized how happy I was to be getting out of that place and going home. Actually, I'd never allowed myself to think of going home for fear I wouldn't have been able to stay once I'd admitted the truth. He gave me a big hug and asked me how I was doing. Then he asked, "What happened to your hair, Noo?"

We both laughed as I put my hand on my plaits in an effort to hide them and shook my head.

Jackie had redone my hair the day before. I don't ever remember wearing my hair the way it felt she plaited it. There were no mirrors so I hadn't actually seen it. But it had to look better than the alternative of having it stick up on top of my head. Dad really would have freaked out if he had seen it uncombed. I was a teenager who was going into the ninth grade, so I had long ago stopped wearing plaits and little girl hair styles.

He took my box and said, "Let's get you home."

We walked out of jail and headed to the street where our station wagon was parked. I staggered as the bright sunlight hit me. I felt light-headed and faint at first as I breathed in the fresh air. I didn't want Dad to know how the sun and air were affecting me, but my knees felt weak. Being cramped in a hot, dark, and dreary cell without proper nutrition for a week had taken a toll on my body, but that was something I definitely had the ability and will to overcome.

I was so surprised to see two of my brothers, Ed and Paul, waiting at the car. They seemed so happy to see me. Once we were in the car and on our way home, my brothers asked me a million questions about what happened while I was in jail. I was careful in responding since Dad was listening. I needed to judge how he felt about me disobeying him and Mama and getting all of us entangled in a legal situation. My stomach started aching as I thought about what punishment I would be given. I knew one was coming and that I had deliberately brought it on myself. I kept talking about jail with my brothers, but I was thinking about my fate.

It took about an hour to reach home. The first thing I saw was Papa Richards and Grandma Belle's car parked in front of the house.

Paul said, "Noo, Grand Vann is here, too."

"Has something happened?" I asked.

Dad looked at me as if he didn't believe my question, saying, "As if you don't know! Everybody has been scared that something would happen to you in jail. After we found out for sure we could post your bond and you could be released today, they decided to come from Cuthbert to see you."

"Wow!" was all I could say. I started thinking how embarrassed I was that everybody was going to see me get punished.

I opened the back door of the station wagon and slowly got out. Mama ran out the house and met me at the car. She hugged me and said how glad she was to see me and have me back home.

I told her I was glad to be home, too, and uttered other similar expressions, but I knew I was walking on eggshells. Dad would sometimes forego punishments or perhaps even forget, but not Mama. She never forgot!

When I walked in the front door, I smelled food and I realized just how hungry I was. My three grandparents were sitting in the living room and they started hugging me and saying how proud they were of me.

I was caught totally off guard.

"They really are proud of you," an inner voice said.

Mama said, "We have a wonderful afternoon planned to welcome you home. First, though, let's get you in the tub for a good bath and get your hair washed. We want you to look pretty for the celebration."

A celebration? Huh? I must have been at the wrong house. I couldn't belong to these people. My mind was racing. I needed to settle down and focus.

I told Mama I needed to call the parents of many of the girls to let them know they are ready to come home.

"It's already taken care of. The movement is notifying parents and paying for those who don't have the money to get their children out."

"How much money do you have to pay?" I asked in a weak voice, knowing I had caused an extra expense on my family.

"It was $10," she said without any sound of regret or strain.

I was so relieved! I thought they might have had to pay hundreds of dollars.

"Mama, she may need to be scrubbed down outside with disinfectants and the water hose before she gets in the bathtub. We don't know what kind of diseases and bugs she may have brought back," Larene said.

"I think it'll be all right this time," Mama laughed.

I was amazed at how lighthearted Mama was being about everything so far. I was still on guard but figured she might wait until after our grandparents left.

I had a very long bath, almost falling asleep in the warm soapy water. Mama let me put on some of her Coty Emeraude dusting powder. This was a real treat! Although the fragrance clashed with my cheap toilet water, I didn't care. I smelled so fresh, and any scent was better than the funky order of the Camilla jail.

Larene didn't seem angry at me and didn't fuss about having to wash my hair. I was so happy about that and felt like I was in heaven. She oiled my hair real good with Vaseline and pulled it to the back in a knot at my neck. Vaseline always made my hair shiny black and wavy. It looked so pretty.

I was now clean from head to toe. I returned to my bedroom to get dressed and was surprised to see a new sun dress laying on my bed and a pair of pretty blue sandals.

I said to myself, "This isn't real. Mama has never, ever, rewarded a defiant child. I'm being set up for a big letdown."

After I was dressed, Momma yelled for me. I jumped to attention and quickly went to her, not wanting to aggravate her and add to my impending punishment. She directed me into what had been the bedroom of two of my brothers. I couldn't believe my eyes. The room had been remodeled. On one wall was a new blue sofa. Facing it on the opposite wall was a table-model television. It sat on one end of our study desk.

"This is our new den," Dad proudly proclaimed as he, too, entered the room.

"Wow," I said over and over.

I couldn't believe all the changes that had been made in just a week. We were now a two-television family. Our other television was still in the living room. It was not exactly a floor model, but it came close. It sat on legs about 8 or 10 inches from the floor and could swivel from side to side. We loved that television and I didn't think it could get any better than that. But now we had a second TV. And we had a den with a new sofa. I learned that the sofa pulled out to a bed and my oldest brother, Vin, had the honor of sleeping on it.

Dad walked over to the new black and white set and adjusted the rabbit ears so that the picture was crystal clear. Lash LaRue and Fuzzy were strategizing about catching a group of outlaws. It was perfect! Lash LaRue was my favorite cowboy. It was because of him that I wanted to be a cowgirl and wear all black. I sat down on that new sofa and began watching the shootout.

"There'll be plenty of time for that later, SavannahBelle. Right now, we are going to have dinner and hear all about your week in jail," Mama said.

I didn't know she would want to hear about my experience. Usually, if you got in trouble, she didn't allow you to explain anything. Usually, she'd say she didn't want to hear a word. She'd just dish out the punishment, and most of the time it would be corporal punishment. Mama was tough!

CHAPTER TWELVE

"Dinner is served," Mama said with a ring of joy in her voice.

The spread of food was unbelievable. If I hadn't been told that this feast was to welcome me back home, I would have thought a king or queen was coming to dinner. There was a big platter of fried chicken, a large sliced beef roast with gravy, string beans, field peas, mashed potatoes, corn on the cob, corn bread muffins, banana pudding, my favorite blackberry cobbler that Grand Vann made, and lemonade.

Mama had set the big table with her gold-trimmed fine china and flatware. She only used these on special occasions. I was in awe! Two smaller tables also were set and all of the tables had table cloths. I had to remind myself that this was not even a Sunday dinner. This was Saturday.

I was told to sit at the big table with Mama, Dad, Grand Vann, Grandma Belle, and Papa Richards. This was a real honor. I decided to take a deep breath and enjoy it, then let the punishment take care of itself later.

Dad prayed, "Lord, we truly are thankful for this day and for all your blessings. We are thankful for this family. We thank you for bringing Noo home without any dog bites and bruises. We pray for the other children to come home **soon.**

These are troubling days, Lord. We know you hear our prayers and pleas. We are leaving it in your hands. And, Lord, bless this dinner that was prepared for our bodies. Thank you for putting food on the shelves and on the table."

Then everyone said a Bible verse.

I said with surprised conviction a verse from the 23rd Psalm, "The Lord is my Shepherd, I shall not want!"

After everybody had recited a Bible verse, Dad said, "Amen. Now let's enjoy this dinner."

I was starved and really had missed the smell of delicious food. As Dad often warned, my eyes were much bigger than my stomach and I put everything on my plate. I was full almost immediately, but nobody chided me about having put so much on my plate.

Soon we were engaged in discussion about the activities of jail and my week away from home. Everybody was genuinely interested in the details, and I found myself recalling details of each day without any hesitation.

They had similar reactions to my description of us sleeping two nights on iron bed frames and tables, of the guards bringing those vicious dogs into the cell and scaring us, of that guard serving us grits with his nasty hands, of the beating of the boys and moving them to another facility, of the fake doctor giving the girls shots of an unknown solution using the same needle, and of the praying and singing that motivated and comforted us. They were in awe about the visit from Dr. King and how he had thanked us for supporting the movement. I didn't tell them about last night's horrifying experience with the monster. I was trying to wipe that from my memory. I probably would tell Larene later.

Grandma Belle said, "I am so proud of you, SavannahBelle. I prayed so hard that you would be safe, and I was scared those hateful police would hurt you. But I also knew the Lord would protect you. So I was glad that you had the gumption to step out and fight for our rights."

Did Grandma Belle just say she was glad I marched? Did she say she was proud of me? Is she for real?

Then Papa Richards joined in, "I thought she was going to keep God tied up the whole time you were locked up, begging Him to take care of you. 'Course, I was praying, too, but Belle didn't ease up none. I'd say 'Hon, don't you think God heard you 10 minutes ago?'"

Everybody started laughing.

"Say what you will, but those were some tense days. I'm not ashamed of how I carried on. God knows when you're hurting and need Him. And didn't He answer my prayers?"

"He was tired of you, Hon," Papa Richards said, again to a roar of laughter.

Grand Vann said, "Belle, you and me both were keeping the line busy in Heaven. You can never pray too much. I always told my boys when they went in service that if you are ever in a situation and can't pray, just raise your finger toward Heaven. The Lord will understand and know what you need. That's what I was hoping SavannahBelle would do if she got in that kind of situation while she was locked in that jail."

I couldn't see Mama's expression and didn't know her reaction to what my grandparents were saying, but I wasn't crazy enough to show how good I was feeling. I didn't want her to think I was being arrogant about my disobedience.

I said, "I believe God heard the prayers from the girls who prayed in jail because they really knew how to pray. They knew just the words to say."

"No, no, baby, there's no such thing as really knowing how to pray. God doesn't measure prayer or answer it by how good it sounds or how fancy the words are. It's what's in your heart. He listens to how sincere you are," Grandma Belle said.

And Grand Vann added, "That is so true, SavannahBelle, and you can get His attention by just asking Him to have mercy on you. Our forefathers didn't have a mastery of the King's English so they couldn't pray all fancy with big words, but what they had was faith. They believed that God would one day rescue them and they held on to that belief. That's what God looks at."

"Yes, ma'am," I said out loud, but I was still thinking about how mature those prayers were. They were not children's prayers.

Papa Richards said, "It's time for a change. As long as we do nothing, White folks will always consider us their property to do as they please. We not slaves no more."

Grand Vann said, "I'll say amen to that. You made me think about an incident when my children were young and Gus was the maintenance man at Andrew College. One day, the president of the college came out on the grounds where Gus was working. He told him they had had a meeting the day before and decided his five boys would be in the May Day parade the college was having the following Saturday. Gus said he asked him what his boys could possibly do in a May Day parade. The president told him to just have them there early that Saturday morning to get ready for the noon parade. He went on to tell Gus that they wanted the boys to ride on a wagon piled high with bales of hay and eat watermelon during the parade route."

My siblings and I fell out laughing trying to imagine our uncles riding on the back of a wagon, sitting on top of hay, eating watermelon in a parade for White folk.

Vin said, "We know that can't be the end of that story because our uncles are no Stepin Fetchits, especially Uncle Bob and Uncle Chris."

Grand Vann chuckled as she continued, "I didn't let Gus finish telling me what else was said before I jumped in and told him, 'Never! They'll ride on a wagon eating watermelon over my dead body!'

"Gus told me to let him finish. He said he told the president that he was afraid his sons wouldn't be able to help them out in the parade, that the three teenage boys worked on Saturdays and the two younger ones had asthma and couldn't breathe around hay.

"You know, I could never have lived with myself if we had allowed our sons to be made fools of like that. Can you imagine, high school boys being paraded around town like clowns and how they would have been teased and laughed at by their friends?"

Daddy Gus, that's what the grandkids called him, was named Augustus Bankston. He worked at Andrew College, a White all-girls college, almost all his life. We were so sad when he died.

Grand Vann said they expected Daddy Gus to be fired after he refused to let the boys be in the parade. He wasn't, and many years later the school dedicated a yearbook in his honor.

"My point is this; you have to stand up for what is right and what you believe in. You have to respect yourself, have dignity. The president told Gus that *they* had decided his boys would be in the parade. That's because they think they own you and you don't have sense enough to say no."

Mama then said, "They ended up asking our principal to pick a few of the high school girls to be in the parade. He was so happy to oblige. He chose six of the lightest-skinned girls in the school. I was in high school at the time, but I just wasn't light enough. Anyway, you can't imagine what they had them do."

"What?" we all asked at once.

"They were told to wear white dresses and shoes and assemble around the May pole when the parade ended. The May pole was across the street from the campus in a big park. Once there, each girl was given a big bright red and green cardboard watermelon slice that the girls at the college made. They were instructed to hold the slice in front of them as they entertained the crowd while doing the 'Watermelon Dance.'"

"Watermelon Dance? I never heard of that dance before. Is that a dance y'all did?" Larene asked.

"We'd never heard of it before, either. The White girls at the college made up some silly steps for them to do as they circled the May pole, and they called it the Watermelon Dance. The girls had to go up to the college a couple of times to be taught the dance but were never told the name until they were given the watermelon slices and introduced at the May Day activity."

"How humiliating and insulting," Larene said shaking her head.

Dad said, "They were determined one way or another to connect watermelon and Negroes. Since they couldn't have the Bankston boys grinning and eating it on a wagon, they had those poor Negro girls carrying a picture of it while shuffling and bowing to them. Why couldn't the White girls carry the picture and dance? It was their doggone school."

Dad was getting angry talking about an incident that had happened more than 20 years before.

"That's why I wanted to be at this dinner to let SavannahBelle know that I'm so glad she stood up for our rights. At 13, she showed courage," Grand Vann concluded.

"Yes, she did," Mama said.

I put my hand over my mouth to contain whatever was churning in my throat about to come full force out of it. I don't know whether it was a wail, sob, gasp, or just plain relief. All I know is that it was coming in a hurry.

Before I knew it, tears were flowing down my cheeks. I was crying so hard my chest began to hurt.

Mama quickly came to my chair and put her arms around me.

"I'm so sorry, Mama. I shouldn't have gone against your rules. I was wrong and I beg you to forgive me."

"You are forgiven. You understand our concern was your safety. But you're home now and that's all that matters."

I felt a ton being lifted from my shoulders. I learned a powerful lesson and vowed never to go against my parents' instructions ever again in life. Worrying about the impending punishment probably was as bad as any they could have given me.

Grandma Belle, in her rich beautiful alto voice, started singing the chorus of her favorite spiritual and all of us joined in:

> *By and by, when the morning comes*
> *All the saints of God are gathered home.*
> *We'll tell the story how we've overcome*
> *For we'll understand it better by and by.*

Then she said, "Let's sing just one verse and end by singing the chorus one more time."

> *We are often destitute of the things that life demands.*
> *Want of food and want of shelter,*
> *thirsty hills and barren lands.*
> *We are trusting in the Lord,*
> *and according to God's Word*
> *We will understand it better by and by.*
>
> *By and by, when the morning comes*
> *All the saints of God are gathered home.*
> *We'll tell the story how we've overcome*
> *For we'll understand it better by and by.*

Between the tears, I was watching Grandma Belle's feet as she sang. She always kept rhythm by lifting her heels. Most of us patted our feet by lifting our toes and the balls of our feet, but she bounced her heels. Whenever I went to church with her, I could almost feel what she described as the Holy Ghost by just listening to the clicking of her heels on the wooden floor. That was the most spiritual combination of sounds I had ever heard: her heels in rhythm with the piano and her golden voice bellowing out those hymns. Even though the sound was different as we sang—we didn't have the piano music and the wooden floor—the spirit was there and I felt so wonderful. This really was a celebration!

After the leftover food was put away and the dishes washed, and I didn't have to lift one finger to help, everyone sat around sharing more stories and laughing at the antics of our parents and grandparents.

I called Bonnie later in the evening. She said that everybody, including the boys, had been released from the Camilla jail by late afternoon. She said the movement had posted bond and sent transportation for those whose families weren't able to do so. I was relieved to hear that. She said that she hadn't slept well on Friday night but slept for several hours on Saturday afternoon and felt much better. I wanted to tell her I hadn't slept well, if at all, on Friday night, either, but that was a conversation I'd rather not have anytime soon. We promised to talk again in a couple of days.

Belinda called to say she was anticipating having our article published in *The Southwest Georgian* newspaper in a couple of weeks. She said she would come to my house on Monday for us to put our notes together. I told her I would be ready.

I went to my room and pulled the dress out of the closet that I had pressed a week ago to wear to church and hung it on the door. In fact, I was anxious to go to Bethel AME Church. I would be listening closely to every prayer, for I now had a new point of reference for serious praying.

Wow! What a day! It was so good to be home. I couldn't wait to sleep in a nice clean bed with a fluffy pillow and smell the fresh sun-dried sheets. I found a new pair of pajamas on my bed when I went into my room. They were from Grandma Belle and Papa Richards.

I was not only forgiven but celebrated. I am truly blessed with a loving family.

Made in the USA
San Bernardino, CA
02 October 2013